Song of Sparrows and Sorrow

Liliana Hart

Original Copyright Sizzle © 2014 by Liliana Hart
Updated Copyright © 2023 by Liliana Hart

All rights reserved.

Published by 7th Press
Dallas, TX 75115

All rights reserved. This book or any portion thereof may not be reproduced or used in any manner whatsoever without the express written permission of the author except for the use of brief quotations in a book review.

This is a work of fiction. Names, characters, businesses, places, events and incidents are either the products of the author's imagination or used in a fictitious manner. Any resemblance to actual persons, living or dead, or actual events is purely coincidental.

Also by Liliana Hart

JJ Graves Mystery Series

Dirty Little Secrets

A Dirty Shame

Dirty Rotten Scoundrel

Down and Dirty

Dirty Deeds

Dirty Laundry

Dirty Money

A Dirty Job

Dirty Devil

Playing Dirty

Dirty Martini

Dirty Dozen

Dirty Minds

Addison Holmes Mystery Series

Whiskey Rebellion

Whiskey Sour

Whiskey For Breakfast

Whiskey, You're The Devil

Whiskey on the Rocks

Whiskey Tango Foxtrot

Whiskey and Gunpowder

Whiskey Lullaby

The Scarlet Chronicles

Bouncing Betty

Hand Grenade Helen

Front Line Francis

The Harley and Davidson Mystery Series

The Farmer's Slaughter

A Tisket a Casket

I Saw Mommy Killing Santa Claus

Get Your Murder Running

Deceased and Desist

Malice in Wonderland

Tequila Mockingbird

Gone With the Sin

Grime and Punishment

Blazing Rattles

A Salt and Battery

Curl Up and Dye

First Comes Death Then Comes Marriage

Box Set 1

Box Set 2

Box Set 3

The Gravediggers

The Darkest Corner

Gone to Dust

Say No More

Outside, you don't hear a single bird, and a deathly, oppressive silence hangs over the house and clings to me as if it were going to drag me into the deepest regions of the underworld…

I wander from room to room, climb up and down the stairs and feel like a songbird whose wings have been ripped off and who keeps hurling itself against the bars of its dark cage.

~Anne Frank

Prologue

Lyon, France
Three years ago

She'd broken all the rules. But boy, had it been worth it.

Eden Kane tried to open her eyes, but they only fluttered before closing again. The effort was too much. Maybe she'd just stay like this forever—her heart pounding, the sweat cooling on her skin, and a very attractive man lying next to her. They were both risking their careers, but love made a person do crazy things.

"I don't think I can move," Jonah Salt murmured against her neck.

"I'm not complaining. I can't feel my legs anyway." Her eyes slowly opened and she noticed some of the candles had guttered out, so the room was cast in shadow instead of a soft yellow glow.

Jonah had been her partner and trainer for the last eight months. He'd been her friend and mentor. He knew her better than anyone else on the planet, and she knew him. And as of tonight, they were husband and wife. The agency was going to lose its collective mind when it found out.

They were covert agents for Oblivion, an off-the-books division of the CIA, and they'd just finished a mission they'd been working for months. It hadn't exactly gone as planned, and now they were waiting to tie up a few loose ends and see what their debriefing orders were.

The small chateau that had been turned into a boutique hotel was where they'd planned to regroup if the mission was compromised. It was high traffic and touristy, and no one would ever suspect that they were anything other than a normal couple. It was an act they'd perfected dozens of times before.

But this time had been different. A romantic atmosphere surrounded them at dinner. The wine had flowed freely. And the love and affection they felt for each other could no longer be hidden or contained. Jonah knew how strict her upbringing had been and how she clung to her beliefs. But she'd been on the verge of compromising them when he'd told her he wanted her to be his wife. He loved and respected her, which wasn't a combination that was always easy to find.

It hadn't taken much for him to use his connections and money to find a priest to marry them quickly. It had been a dream—a surreal moment as she'd promised to love and cherish him forever—knowing the time they had together would be brief before the job called them back.

She could admit the attraction to Jonah had been instant from the moment she laid eyes on him. There was something about the sheer maleness of him that had drawn her in like a moth to flame—a body muscled with years of discipline and determination—calloused hands and the scars of someone who'd lived a lot of life. But it was his eyes that had captivated her—the palest ice blue—intelligent and cunning and wicked at times.

Jonah hadn't been quite so quick to warm to *her* though.

Eden knew her looks made people underestimate her ability, and she accepted her beauty as a tool—a weapon just as deadly as the knife she perpetually wore in her boot. But others, especially men in this business, didn't trust her beauty, thinking there was nothing beneath the surface. So she had to continually prove herself and her abilities, and be better than they were. Jonah had been wary to take her on. But she soon proved her looks were nothing more than a distraction to hide the killer she was beneath.

She'd been Israeli Mossad—one of the elite *Kidon* assassins—before she'd been captured and tortured by the Syrians. All Mossad agents were trained to withstand various torture techniques, and though the training wasn't pleasant, it had kept her from spilling secrets that would have betrayed her country. It was an impressive feat for someone as young as she'd been at the time.

US intelligence agents had rescued her. And she'd been given a choice once she'd been debriefed and made contact with her superiors. She was deemed ineffective by the *Kidon* since she'd been captured, and she had no wish to be one of the numerous intelligence gatherers who did nothing but stare at a computer screen all day. She belonged in the field. So she'd taken the offer the US had given her. A new identity. A new country. A new team.

She'd had no family left in Israel, and though her loyalty had always been to her homeland, she felt the move to the United States was the best she could have made. Her two home countries were allies, and she would defend her new country with honor, just as she had her last.

Her cell phone buzzed—an insistent hum that droned on and on—from the little table across the room. But she was in no hurry to go back to the real world.

"You need to get that?" Jonah asked, kissing the side of her neck before rolling to the other side of the bed. He sat up and ran his fingers through tousled white-blond hair in need of a trim.

"That's my private line, so no. Not until tomorrow. I've got the satellite phone if the agency needs to get in touch."

He stood without any self-consciousness at all, and she watched in pure female appreciation as the muscles in his back flexed as he stretched. Jonah was an interesting man. Quiet in a lot of ways. He was fourteen years older than her own twenty-six years, and what they said about older men being excellent lovers was true. He knew exactly what he was doing, where to touch and taste to make her blood sing. She couldn't have imagined a better first experience. He'd cared for her and loved her—made the moment feel special.

His face was an interesting one rather than handsome. The lines that fanned from his eyes and the corners of his mouth were deep, and his beard was flecked with the occasional strand of white.

"We've got an early morning tomorrow," he said. "The boat will be here to pick us up for debriefing."

Eden sighed and pulled the covers over her chilled skin. "My favorite part. Do you think they're going to be more angry that we didn't get the identity of *Proteus* or that we got married without getting clearance?

Jonah laughed. "You worry too much about the rules."

"Old habits are hard to break," she said. "I still don't understand how everything went so wrong so quickly. Francois Renard was the only person we've been able to find who's had direct contact with *Proteus*. How did they get the explosives in? Renard was right there under surveillance and no one saw anyone else go in or out. We're going to take the rap for his death."

"Maybe a slap on the knuckles," Jonah said, shrugging. "But it wasn't our job to keep Renard alive. It was our job to get him out. Those explosives were well placed and well timed. We're lucky to be alive. In fact, I'm going to be feeling the aches and pains of this mission for a while." He rubbed his hand over the growth of beard on his face and turned to give her a wry smile. "Fieldwork gets harder as you get older."

"If it makes you feel better, I wrenched my knee when we jumped into that drainage ditch."

His eyebrows rose in surprise. "You should have said something. I would have been… gentler." His mouth quirked and she snorted out a laugh. He could always make her laugh.

"Endorphins make an excellent painkiller."

"Hmm, good point," he said. "Don't feel bad about losing Renard. We'll find out who *Proteus* is sooner or later. He's on every worldwide agency's watch list."

Eden licked her lips and debated whether or not to pass along the information she had. He was her partner. Now her husband. And it wasn't that she didn't trust him. She trusted him with her life. But her Mossad training ran deep, and she wasn't used to sharing viable information. She wasn't used to having a partner, period.

Before she could change her mind, she decided to tell him what she'd learned. "I've got a contact from back home. He thinks he's got a line on the identity of *Proteus*, and I've been waiting for him to get in touch."

Jonah's brows shot up. "Really? How did he get close enough to get an identity? Can your informant be trusted?"

"Shai isn't Mossad, but he works special assignments on occasion for the Israeli government as a contractor. He told me he set a trap for *Proteus*. You know how we have that partial recording of *Proteus*'s voice talking to Renard?"

Jonah nodded. "Right, but the voice was distorted."

"Shai is a genius with computers. He didn't care about the voice. He wanted to use the partial set of numbers *Proteus* gave to Renard for payment. Shai was able to use those numbers to find the account. And from there he said it was simple to lay a trap. The next time *Proteus* gets online, Shai will have his identity."

"Very clever of your friend. Good work," he said, nodding approvingly.

"You're not angry at me for keeping it from you?"

"Not at all, love. We all have secrets. Secrets are our line of business. But I'm glad you trusted me enough to tell me. You and I are going to be quite a team." He came toward her and ran his finger down the gentle slope of her jawline. "I knew you'd be mine from the moment I saw you."

"Liar," she said, laughing. "You told me I wouldn't last two days under your training. I believe you also told me there was no place for beauty queens in espionage. I was never a beauty queen, by the way."

"You and that memory of yours. You never forget anything," he said, grinning. "And it looks like I was wrong. You lasted more than two days. Now I can't imagine my life without you in it. My wife."

He leaned down and kissed her softly and she felt her heart sigh. She'd never been in love before, and the feeling was both euphoric and terrifying at the same time. She would go to the ends of the earth for this man. Die for him.

"I'm going to get in the shower," he said. "Care to join me?"

"As tempting as that is, I'm not moving from this spot until morning. I'm exhausted. And I'm not sure my legs are ready for walking."

He kissed her again and moved toward the bathroom. "You do excellent things for a man's ego, love. When should your friend have a lockdown on *Proteus*?"

"The last I heard from him was the day before

we went in for Renard. He said he thought he'd have it within forty-eight hours."

"Excellent. You sure you don't want to join me? I'm feeling very…rejuvenated all of a sudden."

"Yes, I can see that," she said, laughing again. "Why don't you come back here instead?"

"You're a temptress, Agent Kane. But I'm made of stronger stuff than that."

He closed the bathroom door behind him, and Eden snuggled down in the covers as the shower turned on. She smiled as she heard him whistling. The man loved to whistle, especially while they were prepping for a job. It was his thinking mechanism, and she knew once he started whistling she needed to be quiet and let him ponder through possibilities. It was just one of the quirks they'd learned about each other over their time together.

She marveled at the complex creature he was. She'd heard him whistle everything from Metallica to Tchaikovsky. He was currently whistling the theme to *Raiders of the Lost Ark*, making her chuckle. Someone was feeling adventurous.

Wasn't that what love was? Learning each other's idiosyncrasies—likes and dislikes—how to read each other so you knew what your partner wanted without him having to ask?

Her phone buzzed again, but she was lost in her thoughts. She never thought a relationship would be something she could have. She'd been trained from her twelfth year for Mossad, and then at eighteen she'd been selected for the elite *Kidon*. She'd known nothing else. Her future had been determined for her, and she'd always accepted it as it was. There had been no time for dating or thoughts of marriage and family. Only the job.

But Jonah Salt had taken what she'd known and turned it upside down. He'd been her trainer, her friend, and her lover. And now they had to pray that the agency didn't reassign them to opposite sides of the globe in retaliation to their union.

Maybe they needed to keep the secret to themselves awhile longer. Discretion was key and secrets were second nature. Her training had been ingrained and extensive. She could keep her emotions to herself—she'd never cried out once when she'd been tortured by her Syrian captors. And she'd carry the scars on her back and torso forever. But they certainly hadn't bothered Jonah. He had his own share of scars. The scars were just part of who he was, just as hers were part of who she was.

She propped up on her elbow when he came out of the bathroom. A towel was slung low on his hips and droplets of water clung to his skin. He'd shaved and his hair was slicked back from his face.

"It's dangerous to keep looking at me like that, love."

"It's dangerous to make threats if you don't intend to follow through," she said, her voice low and seductive.

Her phone buzzed again and he moved to the table, distracted by the interruption. She could tell by the short length of the buzz that it was a text message instead of a call.

"Can you toss that to me?" she said. "I guess they're not going to leave me alone until I answer."

Jonah picked the phone up from the table and looked at the screen. "Looks like your friend found *Proteus*."

Adrenaline surged through her veins at the information. *Proteus* was one of the most dangerous men in the world. He was the mastermind of too many crimes to count, but there was never enough evidence to pursue. Only statements from witnesses who never managed to survive let them know that he existed at all.

Eden caught the phone with one hand and glanced at the screen, feeling her blood chill at the information there. She looked up in time to watch Jonah pull the trigger.

The fact that the bullet was silenced didn't make it hurt any less when it pierced her chest. The force of it knocked her against the headboard and she struggled to breathe as what felt like molten lead burned through her lungs.

She stared at the face of her partner—her husband—and she knew she couldn't hide her surprise. She'd never suspected. Never thought he could be *Proteus*. And now she'd be dead because of it.

"Surprised, my love?"

She sucked in a breath and heard the whistling sound from her lungs. There was no use trying to speak.

"As you can understand, it's time for me to leave," he said. "You'll have to go through debriefing by yourself. Though I'm not sure they care much at the morgue."

His smile was a slash of cruelty and his eyes were cold as ice. Her lips were wet and she tasted the blood as it bubbled from her mouth.

"Thanks for giving me the name of your informant. I'll take care of him immediately. And thanks for your virginity. There's definitely room for improvement in that area. Maybe in your next life."

Her gun was in the nightstand drawer. She might have a chance if she could just get to it in time, but she wasn't sure she could move her arm. She focused on breathing and put the pain away as she'd been trained to do. Her mind zeroed in on the area of her body where the bullet had pierced, slowing the beat of her heart so her blood didn't pump from the wound quite as fast. She knew how to survive. It was these skills Mossad excelled at over the American agencies.

Jonah began to dress quickly and he started scattering things across the room, tossing tables and their belongings about. But he kept his eye on her. He knew her training better than anyone. Knew that she could be just as deadly while wounded.

Eden's time was running out and she'd never have a better opportunity to try to take him down. She made her move and pulled out the drawer, reaching for the gun inside, but the agony of another bullet had her slumping against the blood-soaked mattress.

"You could never hope to be better than me, love. You're too soft. It's why you failed as a Mossad agent and why you've failed now. Didn't I tell you to never trust anyone? Even your partner? I told you we all have secrets."

She didn't even feel the third bullet as it entered her body. Her eyesight dimmed and the only sound was her waning heartbeat and the soft click of the door as he left her there to die.

Chapter One

Present day

Hospitals reminded him of death—the cloying antiseptic that didn't quite mask the bitter smell of urine and blood, and the insistent beep of machines that pumped life into the fragile human body.

When it came his time to go, he'd rather be taken out swiftly—in the line of duty preferably—without having to linger and waste away while a machine allowed him a few more precious breaths.

Nathan Locke waited patiently as his badge was scanned. A couple of people eyed his weapon nervously, but it would be a cold day in hell before he put his sport coat on to cover it. August in Texas was no joke.

He was finally given clearance to take the elevator to the top floor. His hands were relaxed by his sides, and none of the nerves he felt at being in a hospital were visible. He understood why the meeting had to be here, but he didn't have to like it. Especially since he'd been called back early from vacation. The time spent with his daughter was precious, even more so since it was limited to holidays and summer vacations. But he'd come anyway.

The elevator dinged and the doors opened. The scents and sounds were different here than the rest of the hospital—a highly specialized wing for agency employees, where discretion and anonymity were priority.

It looked more like a hotel than a hospital—the walls were painted a soft green and the rooms were private suites. The carpet, soft and plush beneath his feet, silenced his steps, and he handed his security identification to the nurse at the front desk so she could scribble his name. His mouth quirked in amusement as he noticed she was armed.

It had been eight weeks since Atticus Cameron, the owner of Dynamis Security, had watched his whole world implode. International private security was a dangerous business, especially when it was governments who were hiring the services that only Dynamis could provide.

It was a risk Atticus knew all too well and he'd always taken preventative measures to protect his family. But it was impossible to be everywhere all at once, and he'd been helpless when he'd gotten the call that an unidentified vehicle had opened fire on his wife and daughter as they came out of a movie theater.

He'd buried his wife weeks before. And his daughter, Anna, had been in this hospital since emergency crews had brought her back from the dead. She was still in a coma, having no idea that her mother was dead and her father was barely holding on to his sanity.

But Anna was a fighter and she'd been through more surgeries than most people had in a lifetime. No one knew why she hadn't woken from the coma, but each day that passed was a worry.

Atticus had moved the entire operation of Dynamis to the hospital. He ate, slept and worked there. And Nate knew things must be dire for Atticus to call him while he'd been lounging on a beach in Hawaii with his daughter, Stella, so they'd both hopped on the next flight to Sacramento. His ex-wife had picked up Stella, and then Nate had caught the next leg of his journey to Dallas. He was exhausted, hungry, and irritated by the two hours he'd spent on the runway with a screaming baby two rows behind him. Everyone around him had taken full advantage of the free drinks the flight attendant was giving out. He envied them. But Atticus would expect him to be sober on landing. More's the pity.

The door that led into the suite of rooms Atticus had commandeered was open, but Nate knocked before he stepped inside. Atticus Cameron sat behind a desk that had a view of the Dallas skyline and the pulsing heat that sizzled out from the metal skyscrapers. Atticus commanded this territory as if hospitals were his normal place of business—his laptop open and the sleeves of his shirt rolled to the elbows as he talked softly into his cell phone.

His hair was black as pitch and his eyes like gray fog. One didn't have to look in them long to know he wasn't a man to be messed with. The scar that ran along his jawline only added to the danger that surrounded him. Come to think of it, it might be easy to confuse Atticus for the devil at this particular moment, ruling over the depths of hell if the look on his boss's face was anything to go by.

Atticus nodded at Nate when he came in the room and pointed to one of the chairs in front of the desk.

"You've got two hours," Atticus said to whoever was unfortunate enough to be on the other end of the line. "If I don't hear from Shaw and Peters in two hours and one second, then I'm going to send the forces of hell to come get them and bring them back home. I suggest you don't get in the way."

Atticus hung up the phone and Nate raised his brows. "What happened to Shaw and Peters?" He knew the two agents personally, and he'd worked dozens of missions with them over the last decade or so.

"We lost contact in Kyiv," Atticus said. "Early intelligence is telling us they were betrayed by our contacts there and handed over to a Russian military unit. The Secretary of State is trying to make things political."

Nate laughed. "He doesn't know you very well."

"No, he doesn't," Atticus said. "We'll get them back." He moved from behind the desk and went to the small fridge and took out a couple of waters. He tossed one to Nate and said, "You're looking a little warm."

Nate grimaced. "I don't know how you live here." He was grateful for the water and drank deeply. "I'm pretty sure the soles of my shoes were melting against the pavement."

"I'm told you get used to it," Atticus said. "But I've been here twenty years and I haven't gotten there yet. Thanks for coming in. I'm sorry to cut your vacation short. But as you can see, we're stretched thin at the moment."

"Not a problem." Missing agents was a big deal, and every agent who wasn't on assignment would be needed to help find them. "You know I'd do anything to make sure Shaw and Peters make it back safely."

"How's Stella?"

"Pissed you cut her Hawaiian vacation short," Nate said, grinning at Atticus. "She says you can make it up to her later though. She suggested you give me a raise so I can buy her the car she's been begging for."

Atticus choked out a laugh. The sound was brittle, as if it had been a while since he'd done it. "I can't believe she's driving. Seems like yesterday she was sucking her thumb and asking Jane for a second dessert."

His eyes darkened with grief at the mention of his wife's name. The last time Nate had seen Atticus had been at Jane's funeral. His friend had aged a lifetime in just a few short weeks.

"How's Anna?" Nate looked to the connecting doorway that led to her hospital room. The beep of monitors was soft and he could hear the low hum of cartoons in the background.

Atticus's face said it all—the worry and anguish were plain to see. "Her body is healing. It's a miracle she's alive. You and I have both been shot. We know what it feels like. But for three bullets to ravage her small body is unthinkable."

Nate nodded. "Like you said, a miracle."

"She should have woken up by now. They were able to stop the bleeding on her brain during surgery, but the doctor said sometimes the trauma is so great they choose to stay where they are. It feels safer. I want to see her open her eyes so badly…"

"But?" Nate asked.

Atticus blew out a long breath. "I'm afraid how she'll respond once she remembers what happened to her. What happened to her mother. She's only twelve."

"Anna is a fighter and she's strong. She'll wake up when she's ready. And then the two of you will do whatever it takes to heal. You're a good dad. She'll be okay."

It wasn't often Atticus let his guard down and let his emotions show, but a myriad of expressions crossed his face and tears welled in his eyes. He stood and turned his back so he was facing the window.

"You know I'll do whatever I can to help," Nate said.

Atticus cleared his throat and turned back to his desk, the moment past. He pulled a file from beneath the massive stack of papers on his desk and tossed it to Nate. "Yeah, well, that's why I called you back early. You're the only man I trust for this job."

"Is this about Shaw and Peters?" Nate asked.

"No, I wasn't kidding when I said I'd send the forces of hell to bring them back. I had agents out for a recovery mission the minute I heard they'd been taken. By the time the Secretary of State calls again to tell me why I can't mess up the delicacy of foreign relations, Shaw and Peters will already be back home. No, I need you for a specialized mission. This is classified. It's either you or me. And I'm not leaving here. So you're it."

Nate nodded in understanding. He and

Atticus had come through the ranks together. The two of them had been trained at Langley in experimental black ops missions. The skills they'd been taught were unique, effective, and made people in the American government uneasy. Which was why there'd been some who'd opposed Atticus starting up Dynamis a dozen years before. But his methods were effective, and Atticus could play politics when needed.

"What do you know about Oblivion?" Atticus asked.

"Just whispers really. Only that it exists. It's an off-the-books spook organization. The areas they work are murky at best and always dangerous. Even my security clearance didn't allow for much more information than that."

Atticus nodded as if that's what he expected. "Three years ago, team members of Oblivion were contracted to find and terminate *Proteus*."

Nate let out a low whistle between his teeth and felt his adrenaline surge. He and Atticus had both had run-ins with the terrorist known as *Proteus* in the past. They'd never won against him.

"Oblivion was able to link *Proteus* to a man named Francois Renard. Renard was a broker, and the one *Proteus* most often used. Somehow *Proteus* found out about the link and had Renard taken and held in an abandoned military base in France."

"A leak on the inside?"

"Suspected, but never proven. Oblivion knew Renard had been taken and had a team sent out to observe and assess whether an extraction was possible. It turns out *Proteus* was always a step ahead of the ops team. He'd planned that the team would try to rescue Renard and booby-trapped the whole place with explosives.

"It was run as a standard op. The scouts went in first, taking out guards and clearing the areas. Two agents were assigned to go in specifically for Renard and bring him out. Agents Jonah Salt and Eden Kane."

"Oh, hell." Nate felt his blood run cold. Bits and pieces of what had happened on that mission had trickled to different parts of the agency. It was impossible to keep everything quiet. But they'd done a pretty good job of it. Whatever happened in France had been sealed and buried deep in the CIA vaults.

"Making a long story short, the base was blown to hell and so were most of the agents inside. A couple made it out with critical wounds. Salt and Kane had barely reached the perimeter when the blast went off, no doubt a timing miscalculation on *Proteus*'s part or we'd have found their body parts along with the other agents. They made it out and managed to get back to their safe point to wait for extraction."

"I remember hearing about parts of this before they swept it under the rug." You couldn't belong to the agency without knowing who Jonah Salt was.

"Yeah. The two of them missed their meet for extraction, so undercover agents were dispatched to check out the scene and see what had gone wrong. They found Kane's body. She'd been shot three times in the chest and was hanging on by a thread when the team got there. The room had been ransacked and Salt was nowhere to be found. Kane died twice on the table during surgery."

"But she's alive?"

"She's alive. They never found Salt's body. His car went over the side of a cliff and there wasn't anything left to find. They pulled parts of the wreckage up, but there wasn't enough conclusive evidence to show tampering. There was, however, evidence of another car being involved, an extra pair of skid marks along with Salt's that went to the edge of the cliff. Someone knew who they were and hired a hit on both of them."

"Please tell me you didn't call me in to search for *Proteus*. I'm good, boss, but I think that's a job for more than one man."

"I'd trust you to take *Proteus* out before any of those new recruits they've replaced us with. They're infants. Idiots all of them. They don't make agents like they used to."

Nate grinned. It felt like they'd barely been older than that when they started.

"Anyway," Atticus said. "Proteus is not your assignment. I want you to bring in Eden Kane."

Nate raised a brow in confusion. "Bring her in for what? Isn't she the agency's problem?"

"She resigned her position with the agency while she was still in the hospital recovering. And then as soon as she was able, she disappeared. Oblivion has been looking for her for three years, but not with much enthusiasm. They never got to fully debrief her. They classified her as ineffective, listing cause as severe PTSD and trauma. She was unresponsive for months and they let their guard up. And then she disappeared."

Nate whistled. "And what do you think about her?"

"I think someone with her skill set is never ineffective, no matter the injury or trauma. Her background is impressive. She was Mossad before she was recruited by the agency. *Kidon*."

"You're kidding," Nate said. "And they just let her go?"

"She'd been shot three times and left for dead. And that's after she'd already survived being tortured by the Syrians some years before. The agency is good at tossing things in the trash that don't fit into their box."

"You still haven't told me why you want her."

"I want her at Dynamis. We need another agent and she'll get the freedom here that she never had working for the government. Oblivion might not be worried about what she knows, but she knows something. I've been following her pattern. She's hunting. Trying to stay off the grid as much as possible."

Atticus's smile was sharklike, and Nate let out a short laugh. Atticus could find anyone, anywhere. It didn't matter how off the grid they were.

Atticus handed him a thick file and said, "All of the intel we have is in that file. You'll pick up her trail. Convince her to come back with you."

"And what about this personal mission she seems to be on?"

Atticus shrugged. "Help her if need be. Or see

if she'll abandon it altogether. We need her, and the sooner the better. I'm taking myself out of the field while Anna recovers, and who knows how long Shaw and Peters will be sidelined. Unfortunately, Dynamis has reached the point where I do more good behind a desk than in front of it, so my time is better spent here."

Nate had always admired the way Atticus had balanced his work and his family. Jane and Anna had been the center of his universe. A marriage like Atticus and Jane had was rare. He should know because his own marriage had failed spectacularly. His wife couldn't handle not knowing about the secret missions and worrying about whether he'd come back alive—and he'd been young and arrogant enough to not bother trying to convince her that what they had was worth fighting and working for.

Now his daughter was being raised by another man. Granted, his ex-wife's husband seemed like a good guy and he was good to Stella, but Nate was jealous that the other man was the one getting to see his daughter grow into a woman.

But he'd blown his chance. Which was why Atticus was sending him on this mission and not one of the other agents who had a family. He'd bring Eden Kane back with him and then he'd go on the next mission, and then the next after that. And he wouldn't think about being content. He'd think about surviving.

"I'll bring her in for you," Nate finally said, opening the file. The photograph was taken from her CIA file, but there was nothing ordinary about the woman in it. Her face was clear of cosmetics or any enhancements, and still he had trouble believing what he was seeing.

"Is this some kind of a joke?" Nate asked, uncomfortable at the heat that gathered just beneath his skin and his racing pulse.

"In what way?" Atticus asked, brow arched.

"There's no way this woman was Mossad or working for Oblivion. She'd stick out like a sore thumb. She looks like she should be doing the pageant circuit."

"Interesting," Atticus said, studying him closely. "I guess I didn't notice."

Nate rolled his eyes in irritation. A man would have to be dead not to notice a woman like this one. She wore no makeup in the photo and her dark hair was pulled back in a severe style. But it didn't matter. There was nothing that could detract from beauty like hers. He guessed if he was looking at her critically he'd say her features were unique or arresting—exotic—an oval face with sharp cheekbones and a stubborn chin. A nose that reminded him of a queen he'd seen in an Egyptian relief. Dark brows winged over almond-shaped eyes that reminded him of a raven's feather—a soft black with the slightest tinge of blue.

"Don't be deceived by her looks," Atticus said. "Mossad has a long history of recruiting beautiful and deadly women for just that purpose. I'd pit her skills against yours and mine any day."

Nate sighed. "Why do I have the feeling I'm going to hate this assignment?"

Nate turned the photo facedown, hoping to get the image of her out of his head, but there was another behind it. It took several seconds for him to comprehend what he was seeing.

"God," he whispered. Where her face was a study in sheer beauty, her back was gruesome in its display of cruelty. Thick white scars marred almost every inch of skin where she'd obviously been flogged. Scars on top of scars. And along her ribs the skin was puckered where it had been burned.

"From her time with the Syrians," Atticus explained. "She didn't talk, so the torture went on for almost seventy-two hours before US agents were able to extract her."

Cold fury slid through Nate at the thought of what she'd endured. But he turned to the next photograph, wanting—no needing—to see it all. The next photograph showed the front of her torso. The burn scars extended to the front of her ribs and just beneath her breasts, though her breasts remained untouched and smooth, making the scars seem all the more monstrous.

This photograph must have been the most recent, because three white bandages were placed over the wounds from where she'd been shot. It was a miracle the one in her upper chest hadn't pierced her heart.

Nate nodded and looked at Atticus. "Are you sure about this? This much trauma can damage the mind as well as the body."

Atticus looked beyond him to the room where his daughter lay. "Sometimes it can. But there are special people in the world who are worth pulling out of the abyss. I believe she'll be worth it."

"She's not going to want to come with me. If you say she's hunting, then she's got an agenda and nothing will make her stray from that."

Atticus's lips twitched. "I guess that means you'll be helping her. Call me if there's trouble and I'll spare a couple of extra men, but I think she'll be more agreeable if it's just you. We wouldn't want to scare her off."

"A woman who's been tortured and left for dead isn't likely to scare easily."

Atticus smiled again and the scar along his jaw tightened. "Just make sure you're not the one with your tail tucked between your legs at the end of it. Dynamis Security has a reputation to uphold."

"It takes more than one woman to have me running scared." Nate gave him a two-finger salute and headed toward the elevator. It had been a long time since he'd been on a good hunt.

Chapter Two

For three years, Eden's sole purpose in life had been to track down *Proteus*. And kill him.

She made no excuses for what she'd decided to do. She only knew the man known as *Proteus* had to be stopped. It was easier to think of him as *Proteus* and not Jonah Salt—former mentor and husband. And she'd be lying if she didn't admit that revenge at what he'd done to her weighed in on her decision to take him out. But it was only part of the reason.

He'd put three bullets in her chest, leaving her for dead after she'd given him her trust—something she'd never given lightly and would never give again. To anyone. Then he'd left her for dead and gone for her friend Shai, who'd given her *Proteus*'s identity in the first place. Shai's body had been found in the Jordan River with his throat slit along with evidence of prolonged torture—his back teeth had been missing as well as his genitalia.

Salt had always been a good interrogator, and she had no doubt that by the time he was finished, Shai had given him names of anyone else who knew *Proteus*'s identity, as well as where he kept his computers where the information was stored.

Yes, she wanted revenge. But that was just a side benefit. Salt was a threat to all humankind. And the lives he'd taken, and would continue to take, were why she needed to end him.

No one else had been as close to him as she had. He'd helped train her and had been her partner. Who else would know how to hunt him better than she did?

She'd slipped out from under the agency and gone her own way. And it hadn't been easy, because Jonah was very good at what he did. She liked to think she was better. Like any agent, she had safe houses scattered in different countries that held bags of cash, new identities and weapons. They'd allowed her to survive and blend during her time off the grid.

It had taken her months to recover from the gunshot wounds enough to go out on her own.

They told her she'd died twice on the operating table and was lucky to be alive. She believed in a higher power and understood that she'd been spared so she could finish this last task. Part of her knew she wouldn't come back from this mission alive. And she'd made peace with that.

After leaving the hospital, it had taken another six months to get herself back into shape so she could fight without getting her tail handed to her on a plate. Her body was stronger now than it had even been before her accident, her muscles honed and lean. The scars from the bullets were only another reminder of her mistakes. Mistakes she'd never make again.

It had taken her another six months to get a trace of Jonah's whereabouts. He'd lain low for a while, avoiding most of the terrorist activities *Proteus* had been suspected of. Jonah was arrogant, and that was going to be his downfall. Her patience finally paid off when she'd picked up his trail along the Kamchatka and Russian border.

She had a safe house up in the mountains. It was time to regroup and restock her weapons since she'd had to leave her others behind before crossing the border. She only had the knife in her boot and her fists for protection. It was enough. But one could never be too prepared.

It hadn't been hard to pass through unnoticed. She spoke the language like a native. And no one paid any attention as she started the climb up the mountains to where her safe house was located. She'd only been there once before. Had only needed it once before. But her memory had never failed her.

The weather was brisk and wind slapped at her face the higher into the mountains she climbed. Her jacket was made out of a special material that was thin enough to give her freedom of movement if she needed it, but was as warm as any heavy coat. Neoprene gloves covered her hands for the same reason. They weren't the warmest, but they wouldn't impede her if she needed to fight.

The higher she climbed the quieter it became, and the little hairs on the back of her neck began to stand on end. The temperature had dropped a good thirty degrees and snow crunched beneath her boots as she continued to climb.

There were little signs that most people wouldn't pay attention to—broken twigs or the displacement of small rocks. But she wasn't most people. The mountain was silent, no birds or wildlife to be heard, and because it was silent she walked an extra mile around the perimeter where her cabin was located. She pulled the knife from her boot and waited—just listening—ignoring the white puffs of air that escaped her mouth and the way the cold made her muscles twinge where she'd been wounded.

She crept closer and closer until the cabin was in sight, but she knew by looking at it that Jonah was already gone. He'd definitely been there, though. And he'd left a gift for her to find.

Eden secured the house first, making sure he wasn't waiting to ambush her, before she came back around to the front. The body was placed just in front of the steps of the front door, so she'd have to step over him to get in.

She didn't recognize the victim, only that he'd been a man of some importance. He was dressed in full military regalia and had enough badges and medals pinned to his chest for her to know he'd been in command.

Jonah never did anything without a reason, and leaving the body here was significant, though she wasn't sure why. He'd laid the body out like it would be inside of a casket, with arms crossed over the chest and the ankles crossed as well. His throat had been slit, and the blood had turned the snow beneath him brown. The man's eyes were closed, which meant Jonah had made them that way, and a light dusting of snow covered his eyelashes and hair.

The weather made time of death tricky to pinpoint, but she was guessing the kill was right around twenty-four hours old. Eden had wondered if Jonah would feel her closing in on him. It didn't worry her, but it did complicate matters. Now it would become a game, to see who could outmaneuver the other.

The Russian military would miss this man, whoever he was, which meant she needed to get what she could and get out as fast as possible before she had the Russians on her trail. She didn't have time for another complication.

She left the body where it lay and approached the cabin, stopping in front of the door. The number *165* was written on the lintel, and when she touched her fingers to it, she realized Jonah had used the blood from the man at her feet to write it.

Definitely a game. He was emulating the Passover with the blood over the doorframe because of her Jewish faith, letting her know that this message was meant for her and no other.

Eden reached down and gathered a handful of snow and then rubbed it across the numbers, wiping them away until the snow in her hand melted red. The number would be committed to her memory forever and there was no reason to give whoever would come after her any clues.

The cabin could be wired for explosives. It was a trap she'd considered and discarded. Jonah would want to see this played out and he'd wait before he tried to kill her again. So she was safe. Probably.

She tested the doorknob and found it unlocked, and then she pushed the door wide and stepped inside. It looked exactly as it had the last time she'd seen it. She'd been Mossad then, but a safe house was a safe house. All agents had them, no matter what country they served, and she'd thought this one would be safe from Jonah. She had no idea how he'd found out about it.

The floors were wood and barren, with nothing scattered about to get in the way of an easy exit. A single twin bed was shoved in the corner with blankets folded on top of it. There was canned food in the cupboards and a wood-burning stove.

Eden went to the bed and shoved it across the floor so it screeched against the wood, and she knew by looking at the boards beneath that Jonah had found her stash. But she pried up the loose board anyway and stared down into the empty space.

"Hell."

She grabbed a penlight from her belt and knelt down, shining the light and running her hands along the sides of the small crawl space. She was looking for the next part of his message. Obviously the number *165* was a coordinate, and considering where they were the distance wouldn't be too far. Etched in the dirt in the far corner was the number *66*.

"Not too far away at all." She plugged the numbers she had into her handheld device so it could start searching for possible routes and locations by process of elimination. She stood and dusted off her hands. He'd taken her extra clothes and the main stash of weapons and supplies she'd kept inside.

"I really hate that man."

The cabin groaned and creaked from the cold, settling into itself as she took stock. Annoyance and frustration bit at her and her first thought was to rush through and see if he'd found her reserve stocks, but she held herself back and centered her focus on the room itself. He wanted her to find him, for whatever reason, but he wasn't going to make it easy on her.

"Found you." One of the cupboard doors was ever so slightly ajar. It wasn't noticeable unless you compared it to the order of the rest of the room.

On her way to the cupboard she stopped at the little stone fireplace and stuck her hand up inside it. Her fingers brushed against the gun taped inside the chimney and she ripped it down, at once feeling more at ease with it in her possession.

She held the gun down at her side and approached the cupboard door, edging it the rest of the way open with her finger. And there it was, written in pencil this time. *0800*. And just beneath that was a *51W*.

Eden looked at the watch on her wrist and swore. Wherever she was going she had less than twelve hours to get there. She needed the other coordinate and she needed it fast.

But there was no coordinate to be found. At least not on the inside of the house. She put her gun at the small of her back and stepped back over the body of the man at the base of the outside stairs. Sunset was still a couple of hours off, but she needed to be gone before dark fell and the chances of an ambush rose. She'd prefer not to traverse unfamiliar Russian soil in the middle of the night.

Hers were the only footprints visible in the area. Snow would have fallen between the time Jonah left and when she arrived, making her assumption right that it had been at least twenty-four hours since he'd been there, as snow tended to fall nightly and disappear in the daytime during that time of year.

She made her way to the back of the cabin and the small woodpile stacked waist high. A light sheen of sweat covered her skin as she moved all the wood, exposing the secondary trapdoor she'd built into the ground. She brushed off dead grass and dirt to reveal the rusted iron strongbox she'd buried.

The lid protested as she pulled at it, and eventually gave way with a sound similar to nails on a chalkboard. A sigh of relief she hadn't realized she'd been holding in escaped when she saw the items inside it had been untouched. A secondary cache of money, a new ID, extra hunting knives, a .9mm pistol with an extra magazine, and a long-range rifle.

She worked quickly, outfitting herself for easy access to her weapons, and then assembled the rifle and strapped it to her back. The sun was barely visible above the trees and she still hadn't found the last coordinate marker.

With fierce determination, Eden searched the cabin looking for the last number. She stopped in front of the body Jonah had laid out so precisely and tried to get into the mind of a brilliant criminal.

The position of the body was purposeful. Jonah had laid the man out for burial. The head was facing east, an important detail in many religious ceremonies. She was missing something important.

She knelt by the man and said a small prayer, wishing his soul safe travels into the afterlife, and then she went about the task of searching his body. His hands were empty and there were no marks on his skin discernable to the naked eye. And then her eye caught the glint of metal on his chest, reflected in the last rays of the sun.

"Thirteenth Infantry. 13 North. That should do it."

Now she just had to figure out how to navigate her way across the Bering Strait and make sure she did the last thing Jonah Salt would ever expect.

Chapter Three

It turned out the last thing Jonah would expect her to do was to come in by water.

The coordinates he'd left her led her back into US territory, north of Nome, Alaska. The exact location was in the middle of the water, and there was nothing nearby except oil rigs, tankers, and a smattering of whaling and fishing vessels.

The time frame Jonah had given her had been just enough for her to find a plane and fly herself back into the States. There was one advantage to such an isolated area—it was easy to enter and leave without notice. She landed the seaplane she'd "borrowed" some ways out from shore and used the inflatable life raft in the back of the plane to paddle to shore.

Salt would expect her to come for him by

land, to set up a trap and take him out as he made his way back onto soil. She'd never be as good as him on the water. It was just fact, and he knew it. Jonah had gone through BUD/S training with the SEALs, and was mentally and physically at home at sea. He'd never expect her to come at him from the water. Eden would only have one shot to catch him by surprise.

Stars glittered unusually bright in this part of the world. By Alaska standards, Nome was a large town, but it still had a population of less than four thousand people. She looked through her night-vision goggles, getting the layout of the land. The town itself was nestled on a small flat area of land, but the surrounding areas were hilly and the terrain difficult. A thick covering of snow blanketed everything and it smelled as if more could be coming. She'd be able to assess better in the daylight.

Fishing and whaling boats were scattered haphazardly—different makes, models and sizes—and hooked to rough-hewn docks along the shoreline. They floated lazily in ice-crusted waters, well used and rusted with age. There wasn't much movement in the town, but the docks were already busy with those getting ready to take their boats out.

Eden paid a fisherman named Jerry—who in her opinion needed to head back home and sleep it off—handsomely for the use of his boat. It was smaller than the others along the shoreline, more maneuverable, and the engine sounded smooth and fast when he started it up. Jerry might be a drunk, but he took good care of his equipment.

She set out on the cold and choppy waters, the sea black as pitch, and the stars and a sliver of moon the only light in the sky. Droplets of icy water splashed on her face and clothes and her breath clouded white with every breath she took. The wind cut like a scalpel and made her joints stiff if she stood still too long.

The coordinates Jonah had given her were programmed into her watch, and she turned the engine of the boat off when it buzzed on her wrist, telling her she'd arrived at her destination. She still had half an hour to prep and get set up. Now she only had to wait and watch, and hope she hadn't miscalculated Jonah's expectations of her.

The darkness was both her friend and her enemy. She'd be concealed for a time, giving her the edge she needed. But it would make the shot she'd have to take even more difficult, despite the infrared scope on her rifle.

The long shots weren't her specialty. She could make them, but to be accurate she needed time and intense concentration. Almost perfect conditions. The choppy water and harsh winds were going to be a factor, and she had to make the shot count.

She set up her rifle and scanned the waters through her scope, flexing her fingers to keep them loose. A tanker almost completely concealed the Zodiac anchored next to it. She would've missed it completely if she'd been set up to take the shot on land. That's what he'd been hoping for. He wanted to draw her out. There wasn't a good place for cover on land. There were no trees to speak of and hiding in the hills would've made the distance too great to make an accurate shot.

It was obvious he'd come early to do whatever task he'd assigned himself—nothing good if his past was anything to go by. But Jonah had planned to be finished by the time he'd given her and then he'd expect her to fall into whatever trap he'd set for her. Because he thought he knew her, understood her. When what he'd really done was underestimate the strength of her anger.

The water rippled just before he broke the surface next to the Zodiac and she watched as he rolled in with the experience of hundreds of missions at sea. He spit the rebreather out of his mouth and tossed it in the bottom of the boat. The water and winds were cold, so he kept the neoprene mask pulled down over his face.

She didn't need to see his face. She recognized the way he moved—the relaxed movements that spoke of someone completely at ease in the water. She recognized the breadth of his shoulders and the cruel slash of his smile as he checked the time at his wrist. He was waiting for her, and as if he'd read her mind he picked up his infrared binoculars and looked toward the shore.

He lay flat in the Zodiac and it was then he picked up the rifle that had been lying at the bottom and tried to set his sights on her.

"You son of a bitch." As if her words had carried the distance across the water, he turned and his gaze met hers through the binoculars. She took the shot before he could roll himself back into the water.

She'd aimed for the center of his chest, the largest target she had, but her aim and his movement had altered the course of the bullet and she'd seen it enter his shoulder instead.

Her only hope was that the bullet had hit something vital. She crawled her way back to the engine and started the boat up, not caring that

Jonah could see her now. Gunfire sounded and she heard the ping as a bullet glanced off the side of the boat. She'd gotten him in the right shoulder, so he'd be shooting left-handed. He wasn't as proficient using the other hand, but he was still pretty accurate.

Her only goal was to get back to land. He'd have to spare precious seconds to stop and bind the wound so he didn't lose too much blood, and those seconds were what she needed to make her escape.

At this time of the year, dawn came late and was just rising over the horizon by the time she docked. Sunlight glared in her eyes and off the water, and she wasn't sure she'd ever seen a sunrise quite so bright.

Her adrenaline surged as she hopped down to the rickety dock and used the boat for cover, knowing it wasn't out of the realm of possibility for Jonah to be closer on her trail than she estimated. She still wasn't out of the woods and wouldn't be. Not until Jonah Salt was dead.

Jerry sat in his lawn chair on the snow-covered dock with a blanket spread over his lap and the smell of hundred-proof something reeking out the top of his flask. He eyed the boat and then his gaze went to her and he wheezed out a gin-soaked breath as she passed him another wad of bills as a thank you. She didn't realize until it was too late what had seemed off about Jerry. He'd had guilty eyes.

She felt the air move behind her just before a black sack was tossed over her head. She kicked out blindly, but against so many she knew she was better off saving her energy. Her hands and feet were bound and she was tossed unceremoniously into the back seat of a car. A foot shoved her to the floorboard and then gave her another small kick as someone got into the back seat with her. She heard the distinct sound of a bullet being chambered into a gun and went completely still.

But it was the rapid spatter of Russian that had her breathing out a sigh of relief. It wasn't Jonah who'd found her. At least not yet.

Chapter Four

It had been three weeks since Atticus had passed on the assignment to bring in Eden Kane. Nate had to hand it to Atticus, he never hired anyone who wasn't the best of the best. And Eden Kane was as good as he'd seen.

If he hadn't read her file from cover to cover, memorizing her patterns and trying to get inside her head to see how her mind worked, then he probably never would have found her. And he hated to admit it, but luck had been as much of a factor as his skill with this job. If he hadn't seen her get tossed into the back seat of an SUV, she more than likely would've been long gone by the time he got close enough to make contact.

She'd been alive when they'd bound her hands

and tossed the black cloth bag over her head, so he wasn't particularly worried about her safety for the time being. He was more curious as to why Russian intelligence agents wanted her. It had been a while since he'd used the language, but from his hiding place, and the direction the wind was blowing, he heard and understood enough that they needed Eden. At least for the time being.

Nate waited until the three all-terrain SUVs, one of which had Eden in the back seat, started the drive north. There was only one road in that direction—a two-way stretch most people only used when they were headed to fish in the many rivers around the area. There were some abandoned campgrounds and the remains of a town that had once been popular during the gold rush, but the population had dwindled and the buildings had mostly fallen into disrepair. Only a couple of hundred people called it home now.

Nate waited a couple of minutes and then started up his Humvee to follow behind, turning the heat to high. He hit speed dial on his phone and then set the call to speaker so he could keep his hands free.

"Have you found Eden Kane?" Atticus asked in lieu of greeting.

"You could say that," Nate said. "I just watched a group of Russians toss her into the back of a car and drive away."

"What?" he asked. "That's not good. Russia is not on the table right now."

"Too late," Nate said.

"Where are you? Is she still alive?"

"We're in Alaska," Nate said. "And she's alive. I'm following behind as we speak."

"It wouldn't be good for Dynamis to have any disagreements with Russia. We've got several contracts for services at the moment."

"So noted. I'll make sure I'm not wearing my Dynamis Security T-shirt when I put bullets in them."

"Go get 'em, wise guy," Atticus said and disconnected.

―――

Eden was more irritated than scared at her current predicament.

After an hour-long car ride over a road that felt like it had been made completely of potholes, her legs and hands had fallen asleep. Fighting back would've been a useless effort when they stopped the car and pulled her out by the collar of her shirt. She immediately dropped to her knees since her legs wouldn't support her, and laughter erupted from those who circled her. Snow seeped through her black cargo pants and she was grateful for the neoprene skin suit she wore beneath them.

"Pick her up and bring her inside," one of the men said in Russian. "Stop playing."

Eden's head hung down and the blood was rushing back to her extremities. Her skin prickled like it was being stuck with hot needles. She bit back a groan as they jerked her to her feet and pushed her forward. She'd managed to work her gloves off and she'd started loosening the ropes before she'd lost feeling in her hands, but she hadn't progressed far.

The black bag still covered her head, but she could see pinpricks of sunlight through the fabric. The smell of salt and sea was still strong, though the wind wasn't near as piercing as it had been closer to the shoreline.

Her feet kicked chunks of ice and snow as they led her about fifty yards from the car. The sunlight disappeared, shaded by the building they'd led her to, and she listened as a bolt cutter was used to cut through the lock.

"Hurry. Gregor wants us finished within the hour."

A laugh slithered against her skin and an arm curled around her body as a hand roughly squeezed her breast.

"Have you gotten a look at her face?" the man holding her said. "I'm not going to be done in an hour."

The other men laughed and Eden had to resist the urge to fight against them. It was best to make them think she was weak so she had the advantage of surprise later.

The door slid open noisily, on rails that were in desperate need of oiling, and she felt the rush of air across her skin as it whooshed past. The smell of rotten fish over an underlying odor of motor oil and decaying meat had the gorge rising in the back of her throat, and she had to take a moment to breathe in shallow pants through her mouth.

"Go," he said, shoving her through the opening. The door slid closed behind her with an ominous clank that sent sweat snaking down her spine.

Footsteps crunched over the broken concrete floor and they pushed her farther inside—another thirty steps. They untied her hands and she flexed them to get the blood flowing again and then hands unzipped her jacket and stripped it down her arms. She was left in the long-sleeved black thermal top, but without the jacket there was a noticeable difference in the temperature.

Multiple hands patted her down, taking the weapon at the small of her back, the knife sheathed at her wrist, and the other knife in her boot. They turned her around and shoved her again so the backs of her legs hit something hard, and at the same time hands pushed down on her shoulders so she was sitting in a chair.

Her arms were jerked back, straining the muscles in her shoulders, and they retied her hands. Whoever was tying them wasn't as experienced as the last person because she was able to get her hands in a position where there'd be extra room to maneuver. They bound each of her ankles to a chair leg, and then the bag was jerked off her head.

Eden blinked a couple of times as her eyesight adjusted, and then felt a sharp sting against her face as one of the men backhanded her, snapping her head back. She tasted blood from where her teeth had cut the inside of her cheek and she spat it out at his feet.

"*Kozyol*," he said.

She smiled at the Russian insult and relaxed back against the chair. The ropes that banded her wrists together burned as she worked at them.

She took note of her surroundings, calculating the best route of escape. The warehouse was large, obviously abandoned, and the only light coming in was from the sun shining through broken-out windows and leaving grotesque shadows on the floors.

Old boat parts littered the space and it didn't take her long to find the cause of the awful smell. Whale carcasses were in different stages of decomposition along the side of the warehouse. Natives were allowed to legally hunt and kill a certain number of whales per year for the meat and oil, but the practice was illegal to anyone else. It looked like someone was using the warehouse to hide the contraband.

Windows were spaced evenly on one side, and even though most of the glass was broken out, they were covered by chicken wire and wouldn't be a viable means of escape. There was only one door in and out that she could see. Things were not looking good.

"You've gotten in our way, Ms. Kane," said a

man from the back of the pack. She recognized his voice as the one who'd told the others to stop playing with her. The others moved to either side of her, leaving a direct line of sight between her and the man in charge.

Eden continued to stare at him but didn't say anything. She was as curious for information as they were. He was older than the others and clearly the leader. The scruff on his face was silver, and a black watch cap was pulled low over his head. He'd stripped off his jacket and gloves so he only wore a black T-shirt and cargo pants, which was never a good sign. It meant things were probably going to get messy.

"I've studied you. I know of your past with the man Jonah Salt and that you are hunting him now. Why?"

She continued to stare at him and he smiled before wrapping her hair around his fist and yanking her head back. A knife pricked at her throat and she smelled the coppery tang of blood as the blade bit into her skin.

"I could slit your throat," he whispered, his face so close his whiskers scratched her cheek.

"It would be hard for me to talk if you did," she answered in Russian, turning her head slightly to meet his gaze.

He nodded in what she thought might be approval and moved the knife away slowly. "Yes, well, maybe we should start with other parts of the body. But I've been known to play nice. For instance, my name is Alexsei." He let go of her hair and backed away a step, but he didn't put the knife away. "It is good for a captive to know her captor, wouldn't you agree?"

"It certainly makes it more convenient to track you down later," she said dryly.

He ignored her attempt at humor and began cleaning his fingernails with the tip of his knife. "We've been looking for Jonah Salt for a while now. It was only by chance that we stumbled across you trying to do the same."

Eden arched a brow. What would the Russians want with Jonah? If she voiced the question, she'd owe them an answer. And they'd still probably try to kill her.

"If you're hunting him as well, what does it matter who catches him as long as he's dead?"

"That's the problem. We're not trying to kill him. Jonah Salt's death would be catastrophic for everyone."

"Maybe we're talking about a different Jonah Salt, because from where I'm standing his death could only be good."

The man smiled again and something about it had her blood chilling and her fingers working quicker at the ropes tying her hands.

"I'm telling you now to stop your hunt or you will die here today."

She saw the lie in his eyes. They planned for her to die no matter what she agreed to. It was time to test them, to see what they really wanted with Jonah.

"I guess it's too bad I got a shot off just before you and your goons decided to kidnap me."

"You lie," he spat. Anger and something close to terror crossed his face.

"I'm not. He knew I was tracking him and miscalculated. He was expecting me to come at him from the opposite direction. He knows it'd be risky for me to take a shot from the water. Which is exactly what I did. And I succeeded." The confident smile she gave him did nothing to relieve the tension gathering inside her. Something was very wrong.

"Let me tell you what you've done, *doch' shlyukhi*. Jonah Salt is the Russian Federation's number-one enemy."

The fact that he'd just called her the daughter of a whore barely registered, because she was too surprised by the information he'd just imparted.

If Salt was Russia's number-one enemy, then they were keeping that information to themselves and not reaching out to other agencies to aid in his capture. That was never a good sign.

"As you know, our country relies on the sale of oil, particularly to the United States. Our economy would be devastated without that relationship. And Salt knows this. For the last year he has been holding a few of our tankers hostage. We have many, but he chooses only a handful, arming them with explosives. We do not know which tankers are armed. We only have the demonstration he sent us at the beginning."

Eden's brow furrowed as she tried to recall details of what he might be talking about. And then she remembered. "The Krieg explosion," she said. "An oil tanker off the Pacific waters. The media called it a mini-Exxon Valdez, though the results weren't nearly as widespread. You're saying Salt was responsible?"

"He was. And he's rigged five other vessels. We don't know which ones or even where to begin searching. We only know that as long as we pay Salt his blackmail request of a million dollars per month, then he will not detonate the devices and bring an entire country to ruin."

"Smart of him," she said, thinking the entire

scheme sounded like Jonah. "A steady stream of income. Not enough to draw attention to himself and not enough to break Russia's pocketbook. Very smart."

And horrific. She didn't need Alexsei to explain the ramifications of what would happen if those tankers blew. It'd be a worldwide disaster. Not only the environmental aspects—the effect it would have on water supplies, animals, sea life, and people. But it would also lead to the collapse of Russia's largest resource. An oil spill of that size in five different locations would destroy them.

"So tell me, *sooka*. Did you leave him alive, or did you see him dead?"

"I'm getting tired of the name-calling, Alexsei. And here I thought we were friends." Eden thought quickly. Time was of the essence and there was no reason for her to hold information back from the Russians. It wasn't just their world that was in danger.

"You try my patience," he said, turning the knife in his hand. "I can either call you names or start cutting on your very delectable body."

"Fair enough," she said. "It was a shoulder shot, and it looked clean as far as I could tell. I'm not saying he couldn't succumb to blood loss or infection, but it wasn't a kill shot."

Alexsei nodded and gestured for two of his men to leave, presumably to start the search for a wounded Salt and save his worthless life. What hadn't come out in this conversation was the name of *Proteus*. She was starting to think that bit of information was her secret to keep. It was a bitter pill to swallow, knowing she'd have to save a man she'd wanted nothing more than to see dead.

Alexsei looked at her one last time and then to the men who still flanked her. "Kill her. And be quick about it."

Two men approached her from each side, one of them pulling his knife from the sheath at his waist just as the rope gave way on her wrists. She grabbed them by the shirtfronts and knocked their heads together, catching them both off guard with her freedom.

The knife slipped from one of the men's hands and she caught it, leaning down and cutting the rope wrapped around one of her ankles in one smooth motion. By this time, the other men standing around had recovered their surprise and were circling in. She didn't waste time and threw the knife at Alexsei, hitting him in the throat, and taking out the biggest threat first. The others she could deal with.

Eden used one of the fallen men as leverage

and swung her leg out, the chair still tied to one ankle so it swung in a wide arc, slamming it against two more men with a satisfying crunch against their heads.

The last man came in low and fast and caught her around the middle, but the balance of the chair tied to her leg threw them both off and gave her time for her fingers to find the pressure points in his neck and render him unconscious.

His body collapsed on top of hers, releasing the air in her lungs in a great *whoosh* so she had to fight to suck in another breath. Her ankle was throbbing and her jaw sore, and who knew how many other little aches and pains would make themselves known in the next few hours.

She shoved the body aside and untied the remaining rope from around her ankle, flexing it quickly before she rolled to stand on her feet. Time was of the essence. There would be more Russians to deal with, and the ones littering the ground around her would be waking before too long. Except for Alexsei, whose eyes stared blankly at the ceiling.

It was up to her to find Jonah and see if she could put a stop to his insanity. And if she had to save his life to do so, then so be it. She could always kill him after she had the codes to disarm the explosives on the tankers. She was still the best person for the job to find him and corner him like the rabid animal he was.

Eden leaned down and searched the body nearest to her, relieving him of the gun and knife he'd confiscated from her earlier. Her back was to the door, and though she didn't hear a sound, she knew someone was there—could feel their presence in the shift in the air—and the little prickles of awareness rolled across her skin.

Without warning, she turned and aimed the gun at the intruder. A quirked eyebrow and a cocky grin were all she got in return, and he immediately held his hands up in a sign of peace.

"Don't shoot," he said, the humor still lurking.

She recognized him for what he was—trained to fight. The only question was, who was he fighting for?

He was several inches taller than she was, with the kind of light blond hair that most women could only achieve with a bottle, but she could tell his was perfectly natural. Thick brows were a shade darker in color, and even from where she stood she could see his eyes were as dark as her own. It was an unusual combination. An arresting combination that made her distrust her instincts.

His body was lean and muscled, and he wore

black BDUs and a black jacket very similar to her own. He carried himself like a man who was familiar with every aspect of his body, comfortable in his own skin, and confident in what he could do with the muscles beneath.

He was balanced on the balls of his feet and she knew he wouldn't make it easy for her if she decided to fight her way out.

"Well," he said, looking at the scatter of bodies. "This is a hell of a mess. I hope you left at least one of them alive." He started to drop his hands back to his sides.

"Keep your hands up," she demanded, keeping the gun trained on him.

His grin got wider and a flutter of a dimple teased one side of his mouth, but he didn't keep his hands raised. "I've never been very good at following orders. You won't shoot me."

"I just pulled the trigger on a man who probably thought much the same thing. Why is it that men always underestimate what a woman is capable of?"

His face turned serious and a little bit grim. "I've read your file. I would never think of underestimating you." He said it with such conviction she thought he actually might be telling the truth.

"You're agency then." She nodded, her suspicions suddenly confirmed. "I'm not interested in coming back. Sorry you had to make the trip. But you're going to want to get out of my way. I'm in a hurry."

"I guess it's a good thing I'm here to help you. I've been known to move fast from time to time."

"I don't need help. And if you don't move aside I'm going to put a bullet in you just on principle."

"That would make my daughter unhappy. She doesn't like it when I get shot."

Eden let out a sigh and let the gun drop down to her side. "You're determined to be a pain in my neck, aren't you?"

"I guess that's why my boss sent me for you. Though I don't know what the hell Atticus hopes to do with you. And I overheard enough of the conversation between you and your comrades to know you're going to need help. As far as everyone on the planet is concerned, Jonah Salt died in France. You, me, and the Russians are the only ones who know differently. Tracking Jonah Salt won't be a cakewalk. But I can help you."

"You said Atticus." Her gaze narrowed on him. "Atticus Cameron?"

"Good." He nodded. "It helps speed things up that you've heard of him."

"Of course I've heard of him. Even when I was Mossad I knew who he was. Not to mention he's been trying to track me down for the last year or so. He's persistent, I'll give him that. He's left messages for me all over hell and back to return his calls. He's a hard man to ignore. But I've managed."

"I'll make sure to tell him *someone* was successful at ignoring him," he said dryly.

Her lips wanted to twitch at the obvious good humor on the man's face when he spoke of Atticus, but she forced herself to remain impassive. Emotions had no place in the field. That's what had gotten her into trouble the last time.

"Make yourself useful and help me tie them up. I'd like to get at least a little bit of a head start before they come after me."

"I live to serve," he said.

Eden held the gun on him as he made short work of binding the Russians' hands and feet, and then she made a motion with her weapon for him to move back outside. She leaned down and grabbed her jacket and then followed behind him, keeping her weapon ready just in case her instincts were off and he really was there to kill her. But her gut wasn't tingling, and she thought he might really be there to do as he said.

Once they were outside and a good distance away from the warehouse, he turned and leaned casually against the hood of a Humvee.

"So why did the great Atticus Cameron send you to find me?" she asked.

"You've just been recruited by Dynamis Security. Congratulations and welcome to the team. And I wouldn't even consider saying no. If you know Atticus's reputation then you know he pretty much always gets what he wants. I'm sure there's some kind of paperwork you'll need to fill out. Life insurance policies and all that," he said, grinning. "But as of this moment you're on payroll, so it's probably a good thing you only killed one of those Russians."

Eden narrowed her eyes and tried to sift through all the possible scenarios of what could happen. And then she decided maybe she could use this man's help after all. At least for a little while. Dynamis Security had a lot of power and unlimited resources.

"Do you have a name, or are you just Atticus Cameron's mouthpiece?"

"Nate Locke," he said, holding out a hand for

her to shake. "And sweetheart, I'm nobody's mouthpiece."

Before Eden had time to blink he moved in fast, twisting the gun out of her hand. She countered the move, pivoting in the opposite direction. Their bodies were close enough that she could feel the heat of him as they went through the dance of close combat. He hit the small button on the side of the gun while she still held it and the magazine dropped into his hand. He pulled back the slide and ejected the bullet, letting it fall silently into the snow. Both of her arms were restrained and she was left defenseless—not unless she wanted to really hurt him—and the entire time he never once took his eyes from hers.

Her breath came in short pants, the blood drained from her face, and she immediately released her hold on the gun and fought to get out of his grasp. She hated being restrained, and she fought against the panic.

Nate immediately let her go and looked at her curiously. He held the gun out to her, butt end first. "You ready to go?" he asked as if nothing was out of the normal.

Eden took the gun and then held her hand out for the magazine, wondering if he'd give it to her. He placed it in her hand, looking at her with those dark eyes, and trusting her not to kill him. She wasn't sure if she could've done the same. So she took the magazine and popped it back in before returning the weapon to the small of her back.

And then she did what she'd swore she'd never do again—take on another partner. "Let's go."

Chapter Five

Cold winds blew bitterly, cutting straight through the body and into the soul. Still, Eden preferred the Alaska cold over Russia any day of the week. There was a wild, untamed beauty about the land that inspired a mix of awe, fear, and respect.

Rolling hills of white went for as far as the eye could see, and in the background were snowy mountains that peaked straight into the clouds. Frozen rivers and streams jutted off in all directions, and she bet it was beautiful once the weather warmed and there was color. But for now it was a frozen palace of snow and ice, isolating and eerily quiet in its solitude.

There was nothing *but* solitude.

"This isn't going to be easy," she said as Nate

retraced their route back to the docks where she'd been taken—where she'd fired the shot at Jonah. "There's so much empty space here. It's the perfect place to disappear. And it's snowing again. If we don't hurry all the tracks will be gone."

"It's hard to disappear with a bullet wound and dripping blood everywhere. We'll find him."

Eden hadn't relaxed since she'd gotten in the car with Nate. She'd gotten on the phone with Atticus Cameron at Dynamis as soon as Nate had dialed the number for her. He'd assured her that Nathan Locke was exactly who he said he was. But still…the car ride had been filled with uncomfortable silence, and she'd sat coiled and ready for whatever awaited her.

"You were lovers," Nate said after a few more minutes of silence. "You and Salt."

"That's none of your business. We should be getting close to the docks. I was only in the car for an hour or so."

"I told you I read your file." He completely ignored her attempt to change the subject and her shoulders tensed as she sat up straighter in the passenger seat. "It doesn't take much deductive work to figure out from the way you were found and your medicals that you were closer than partners. And now that I know he's alive, I can deduce that he's the one who shot you. That's cold. No wonder you're out for blood."

"Thank you, Agent Locke, for that analysis," she said, her voice as frigid and brittle as the wind outside.

She heard his sigh and ran through scenarios of how he could use the information against her. In their line of work, information was power.

"I just want you to know I understand what it took for you to come with me. To agree to work with someone again. To hell with Jonah Salt. He's got his own agenda and never intended to utilize your talents. His only thought was to use you how he saw fit. But he underestimated the agent you are."

Eden turned to look at him and found his dark gaze steady and intent on hers. There it was again. That connection that inexplicably linked two people who'd never met and made it seem like they'd known each other forever. He was the one that broke the spell this time as he focused back on the road.

"If he'd bothered to read your file from front to back, he'd have known what a mistake it was to let you live once he'd gotten the word you'd survived his first attempt to kill you. Your profile suggests you don't quit until the job is done. It's you who's going to stop him in the end. I believe that with every instinct in my body."

If Eden had the ability to cry, she might have in that moment. She felt the burn behind her eyes, but no tears formed. She hadn't felt anything but hate since she'd died on that operating table. It had been too long since she'd been around people, and she realized how she must seem to someone like Nate Locke.

He seemed to be fairly laid back with an easy temperament. He took situations as they came, but he was also able to assess them quickly. She hadn't seen how he worked yet and she didn't know his skills, other than his quick display back at the warehouse, but she knew the reputation of Dynamis Security. Atticus Cameron only hired the best agents, so Nate, whatever his skills, was no slacker and he wasn't someone to underestimate.

To him, she probably seemed like a madwoman—cold, brittle, and scorned. A loose cannon if ever there was one. And if she'd been Nate, she'd wonder why her boss was sending her on a wild-goose chase to recruit an agent who was hell bent on vengeance.

But she was still human. And though she

didn't want them, she had feelings and understood that Nate was extending an olive branch of sorts. She wasn't cold, and she missed human contact.

"Thank you," she said softly. And that was all that had to be said. She relaxed and felt the tension leave her shoulders as they made the rest of the drive to the docks.

It was past noon by the time Nate parked the Humvee at the edge of the docks. The snow was falling harder now and they maybe had an hour before all the tracks were covered.

There was no sign of the Russians, so they'd probably come and gone. The longer she and Nate spent retracing their steps, the farther behind Jonah they'd be, and it wouldn't be long before more Russian agents appeared.

"The docks are pretty deserted," Nate said, grabbing a pair of binoculars to look farther down the shoreline.

Eden saw the tanker in the distance where she'd taken the shot at Jonah. It had traveled a good distance, but was still visible to the naked eye. She knew now there was an explosive device somewhere underneath.

"That's the tanker where I found Jonah this morning."

"We'll leave it as is for now. Jonah probably has sensors near the explosives and we don't want him to detonate if he thinks there's a team down there trying to disarm it. I'll pass the information along to Atticus and let him make the call. Come on. Let's go see if anyone remembers seeing anything."

Gray clouds grew thicker as the snow fell—bulging and obese, they looked as if their seams were ready to split and dump white powder over the entire town until it was buried to the rooftops. She pulled a black ski cap over her hair and realized there was nothing she could do to cover the bruise forming on the side of her face. It throbbed painfully, but there was nothing to be done for it.

"I wouldn't mind paying a visit to my good friend fisher Jerry that sold me out to the Russians," she said, narrowing her eyes.

"If you could see your face right now. Remind me not to get on your bad side." Nate grinned and pulled on his own watch cap and then the hood of his jacket over that. "I'd be shaking in my fisher boots if I was him."

She groaned before she could help it and rolled her eyes. "You can't be for real. Atticus would not hire an idiot for his team."

"Just remember that, sweetheart, and we'll be good to go. I've learned in this business you have to take your pleasures where you can. Otherwise you'll burn out and end up eating your own bullet. Besides, I'm a dad. I'm honor bound to tell the occasional dad joke."

Nate grabbed a pistol from beneath his seat and got out of the Humvee, putting it at the small of his back, and she did the same.

"Oh, and Nate." Eden waited until he turned to give her his full attention. "The next time you call me sweetheart I'm going to put a bullet in your kneecap. I'm not a fan of endearments." Not since Jonah Salt had used them so freely.

"Make sure you shoot for my left knee. The cartilage is already worn to hell and back and I've heard the R&D lab at Dynamis can give me a new bionic one."

He turned away from her and started walking toward the docks. Eden blew out a breath. She had no idea how to handle Nate Locke, and it was disturbing to say the least.

"Hell," she said under her breath and followed after him.

Her eyes were never still, tracking the roads and possible hiding places where Jonah or the Russians could be waiting to ambush them. Nate had been right. The docks were all but deserted at this time of the day, but there was a kid of about nineteen or twenty looping rope in a figure eight pattern around two wooden posts up on a boat.

"Hey, man," Nate called out. "Can I talk to you for a minute?"

The kid looked up from his ropes. His face was pockmarked with acne scars and a red bandana was tied around his head to keep his long hair out of his eyes.

"Time's money, man." And then he went back to his rope.

"So it is." Nate pulled out his wallet and a couple of twenties and the kid let the rope fall. He jumped over the side of the boat and landed in front of them on the dock with the surefootedness of someone who spent most of their time at sea. He held out his hand for the money.

"Information first," Nate said, making the kid grin and shrug. "How long have you been hanging around today?"

"My old man and me take tourists out for fishing. We had clients this morning that paid big bucks to wake up early and freeze their tails off just so they could take a picture with a fish half their size and hang it in an office on Wall Street somewhere. But we had to cancel the trip and reschedule for tomorrow.

"Denny, he's the police chief. He came by with a few other cops and said a couple tourists saw a lady get kidnapped this morning. The tourists were making a stink about it so Denny and the others made all the boats stay docked so they could search them for the woman."

"Did they find her?"

"Nah, it was bogus. Old Jerry told them they was crazy. That's his boat down there," he said, pointing to the boat Eden had taken out that morning to search for Jonah. Her face didn't betray her feelings. It wasn't the kid's fault old Jerry was a two-timing worm.

"Jerry told them it must have been a crank call cause nothing but fishing and tourist-type stuff goes on down at these docks. We all make our living from the water, and a day wasted is money gone. Which is why if you want more information you're going to have to add another twenty."

Nate peeled off two more twenties and a picture out of the inside pocket of his jacket. "Did you happen to see this man hanging around this morning? It's possible he was hurt."

The kid stared at the photo and then shrugged. "I don't know, man, it was dark. Only thing weird I saw this morning was a yellow Zodiac heading north up the shoreline. Didn't pay much attention to it. Figured it might have been one of the guys unloading some drugs or something before the cops boarded the boats. We've got cargo planes going in and out all the time bringing stuff in and taking it out again. I wouldn't be surprised if not all of it was legal."

Nate passed over the money. "I don't suppose old Jerry is still around for the day?"

"Nah, dude went home sick after the cops left. Didn't look good at all. He's a drunk, so I figure he had a bad night."

"Thanks for your help, man." The kid scurried up the rope ladder and was back on deck before they'd turned to walk away.

"Lucky for old Jerry he got sick," Eden said as they headed back toward the Humvee.

"Let's follow the north road for as long as we can and see if we can find the Zodiac. Salt will have dumped it and had a contingency plan of some kind. You know he was probably here almost twenty-four hours before you arrived."

They got back in the Humvee and he started it up, backtracking the way they'd come and following the coast road that would eventually dead-end. All of the roads out of Nome led to nowhere. It was well and truly isolated unless you had means to traverse the land in other ways.

"What will he do next?" Nate asked. "Tell me your gut feeling."

He'd do exactly what Eden was afraid he might do. He was going to disappear. "He's wounded, but he won't need help. He's trained in medical and he'll know what to do to patch himself up. You're right. He was here long enough to gather supplies and set up transportation. He'd have to do it here in town though, so we can check that out if we lose his trail. He's going to disappear right in front of our faces. He'll use the land and his skills to live until he thinks it's safe to head somewhere else."

"Don't forget the Russians," Nate said. "We're not the only ones looking for him. And they're going to be looking for *us* too. Salt is going to need access to the internet, otherwise his blackmail scheme isn't going to work. And as much as we like to think it isn't so, technology is the best way to find someone."

"Say we find Jonah. How are we going to disarm the bombs on those tankers without him blowing them first? He'll have detonation codes and there's no way in hell he'll be giving them to us."

"That's the million-dollar question, sweet—" Nate looked at her sheepishly out of the corner of his eye and grinned. "Agent Kane."

"And your bionic knee is put on hold another day." She felt her lips twitch and looked out the window to hide it.

"In all seriousness, when we get to that point, that's when you're going to be glad Dynamis Security is on your side. Calvin Cruz is one of the best computer hackers I've ever known. It makes the CIA and the Pentagon really nervous that he's working for Dynamis and not in their own house."

"Never heard of him," she said.

"Most people only know of him as Cypher."

"Right," Eden said, impressed. "Him I've heard of." And the fact that Dynamis Security had acquired someone who was considered as much of a threat as a hero for all the good he'd done for the country said something. Cypher was a man of many talents. It only made her more curious about the man sitting next to her and what he was hiding.

"Look there," he said, pulling to the side of the road. "Tracks in the snow. Multiple sets by the looks of it."

He left the engine running and they both got out, leaving the doors open in case they needed cover. Eden's gun was out and she automatically covered Nate's back as they looked around for any unseen threats. The land was open and there wasn't a good place for cover, so they both relaxed and focused on the tracks that were quickly being filled in.

"Blood," Nate said, bending down in the road to get a closer look.

"He tried to cover his tracks, sweeping behind himself, but he took a direct hit. There's no way he didn't leave blood behind. Looks like we found where he came back on land."

"And there's the Zodiac."

There was a steep drop from the road to the shoreline and Nate stood right at the edge looking down. The Zodiac, or what was left of it, rippled like ribbons in the water, caught on some kind of plant. Jonah had taken his knife to it to help it sink faster, but it would've still been dark when he'd come ashore and he'd have been in a hurry.

"He's making mistakes," she said. "He could be hurt worse than I thought."

"If he's made one, he'll make others. He had some kind of vehicle parked here on the road so he could get out easily."

"It looks like a snowmobile or something similar. The tracks are odd. The other set of tires are going to be from our Russian friends."

"Let's follow the trail for as long as we can, then we'll need to stop and regroup and pick up some supplies. I'll need to check in with Atticus too."

Eden looked over at him and arched a brow. "And how are your survivalist skills, Agent Locke?"

He went back to the Humvee, but she saw his mouth twitch. "They're passable. You won't have to haul me through the snow on your back, if that's what you're wondering."

"Don't worry. I'd just leave you to the scavengers. Wolves get awful hungry this time of year." She had to admit she enjoyed bantering with him. And he might not know it, but if she had to she'd haul him out of hell. Because that's what partners did. And until he proved otherwise, that's just what he was, and she'd already begun to think of him that way.

"You have a mean streak," he said, putting the Humvee in drive and following the tracks left in the road. "I don't know why I like that about you."

The laugh took her by surprise. It had been so long since she'd done it she almost didn't recognize the sound that had come from her throat.

"You know, neither you nor Atticus mentioned what your background was. Were you military or CIA? I don't remember ever hearing the name Nate Locke whispered among the legends."

"What can I say, I'm a private kind of guy."

"Legend said that Atticus Cameron always worked with the same team. Cypher was one of those people. Gabe Brennan was another."

"Gabe Brennan has opened his own security agency on the European side of things. He and Atticus still work together on occasion."

"Damian Huxley was also in his band of merry men."

"Yeah, well, Huxley turned out to be as big a bastard as Jonah Salt. You're not the only one who's been betrayed by someone you thought you could trust. By a friend you've known most of your life. Atticus lost his wife and his daughter is hanging on by a thread because of Huxley."

"I'm sorry," she said. "I hadn't heard. I've been off-grid for the last few months."

Eden tilted her head and looked closely at him. He didn't give anything away. There was no emotion on his face. No outward signs that he was uncomfortable talking about the subject. But her gut told her there was more there than he was letting on.

"Yeah, well, Huxley is dead so that's something at least."

"Vengeance is sweet," she said in agreement. "If I recall, there was a fifth man on Atticus's team. A guy only known as Warlock. I don't recall ever hearing what happened to him. Does he work for Dynamis?"

Nate braked and brought the Humvee to an easy stop in the road. Visibility was becoming more difficult by the second and the tracks had all but disappeared. They were going to have to stop and turn back until things cleared up.

She kept looking at him, waiting for—something. Something that would give her a clue about the man she was entrusting her life to.

He put the Humvee in reverse and did a three-point turn to take them back into town, but he stopped and looked at her, his face unusually serious. She hadn't really realized until that moment how his face had always been filled with such good humor. She wondered now if it was a mask to hide something darker.

"You know him?" she finally asked, after the tension dragged on.

He shook his head and turned back to the road. "Never heard of him."

Chapter Six

The Humvee crept along the road and the windows strained as the wind blew off the water, and Nate kept his grip relaxed against the wheel, despite the pounding need in him to squeeze it hard enough to make his hands ache.

He had no idea what had just happened, but Eden Kane was more perceptive than he'd given her credit for. Just because she'd isolated herself the last couple of years didn't mean she'd forgotten how to read someone.

It had been years since he'd heard the name Warlock—for good reason. Warlock had been killed in Russia. And because Warlock had died, Nate Locke had been able to live out in the open and without fear that someone would try to hunt him down. Cypher had made sure that all mentions of Warlock and Nate Locke being one and the same had been erased from history. It was still possible his past could catch up to him at some point, but it was unlikely. Cypher was the best.

Warlock had seen and done things for his country that ate holes in his gut if he thought about them too long. The memories still plagued him in nightmares, which was only one of the reasons he'd chosen to remain single. Most women didn't care to be woken out of a sound sleep by a man screaming as if being skinned alive by Satan himself.

He'd have to be very careful with Eden and make sure she didn't find out the truth about the monster he'd been, and why it had been so important for him to die and start over again.

Snow blew so hard into the windshield that it was impossible to see anything but white, so Nate almost hit the man standing in the middle of the road before he saw him. He slammed on the brakes and was thankful he hadn't been going very fast to begin with. Eden had her gun out and pointed at the windshield before he'd come to a complete stop.

Nate was about to slam the car in reverse when the man's hands came up in front of him, palms out in a gesture to signal they stop. A heavy coat lined with fur dwarfed him, and a fur-lined hood surrounded his face. And then between swishes of the wipers, he was gone as quickly as he appeared.

"What the hell—" Eden said, bringing her gun down.

The knock on Nate's window had both of their weapons coming up and their adrenaline spiking. The old man's face was all but pressed up to the glass, brown and wrinkled with age, most of his teeth missing as he smiled a jack-o'-lantern smile. Snow gathered on his eyebrows and lashes and gray hair hung in long braids on both sides of his face. Nate released the breath he'd been holding and put his gun in his lap, though he kept his hand on it.

"Holy hell," Eden said, releasing her own breath. "That was creepy. What does he want?"

"Let's find out." Nate rolled down the window and snow blew into the car, slapping and stinging against his face.

"Atticus Cameron sent me," the old man said, his Native accent thick but not difficult to understand. He eyed the gun Eden pointed at him with curiosity and then turned back to Nate, dismissing the threat. "I'll ride in back and you can take me to town. This weather is only going to get worse, and I'm old."

No kidding, Nate thought. The man had to be about the oldest person he'd ever seen. He sighed and hit the lock switch so the man could get in.

The man moved to the back door and Nate whispered, "Of course Atticus sent him. Only Atticus would send the oldest man in the universe to help us. He's probably sitting at home, laughing his head off."

"Atticus doesn't strike me as the type of guy to have much of a sense of humor," Eden said.

She watched the man closely as he got into the back seat, and Nate noticed she didn't take her weapon off him, though she did relax her grip some.

"Oh, Atticus is a very funny guy," the man said, nodding. "A real prankster."

"That's very true," Nate said. "Or at least he used to be. Why did Atticus send you?"

"He said you need supplies. I have supplies." The man shrugged and threw his hands up, sending droplets of water throughout the car.

"Simple fix. You will stay with me until the storm clears. My name is Chanlyeya, but everyone calls me Joe."

Nate knew when to not argue, and he'd stopped questioning long ago how Atticus knew before his agents did when they were going to need something. He had contingency plans on top of contingency plans.

"The man you are after will not get far. The storm is too bad. And the two men after him will not get far either. Plenty of time. I am wise and old. You will listen to me. You hungry?"

"I could eat," Nate said, pressing on the gas pedal.

"You drive like an old woman," Joe said. "We'll not get there until tonight. Pedal to the metal, friend. I'll be your eyes."

Nate gritted his teeth and ignored Eden's snicker from the passenger seat. So *now* she decided to get her sense of humor back. He did the only thing he could to save face and pushed on the gas, the Humvee fishtailing once before righting itself and speeding ahead.

Strangely enough, using Joe's eyes worked pretty well and Nate just followed his directions until they got back to town.

"Stop here," Joe said. "No point in going farther. You won't be using a car again for many days. The snow will cover them all by morning."

"It's too bad Jonah didn't choose Key West for this little adventure," Eden muttered under her breath. "I wouldn't mind a little sun and sand right about now."

"I was in Afghanistan for a while," Nate said. "Sand is overrated if there isn't a beach to accompany it. I've probably still got sand in places I don't care to mention."

"Maybe one day you'll find a pearl in your shorts," Joe said, his grin gap-toothed.

This time Eden laughed out loud and slapped her hand over her mouth to keep it inside. Nate could tell she'd surprised herself by the action, and if he could give her that then he'd let Joe make fun of him all he wanted.

"Is your house close?" he asked, pushing open the car door and stepping out into the wind and snow.

"Close enough." Joe pulled the hood back up over his braids, but he didn't seem to be bothered by the cold.

Eden's lips were pressed tight together as she tried to keep her teeth from chattering. She zipped her jacket up to her neck and pulled her hat low. They were going to need more gear if they were going to follow Jonah across Alaska. She hoped Joe could do as he'd promised Atticus.

Nate retrieved his duffle bag from the back and realized Eden didn't have anything but the weapons on her. As if reading his mind she said, "I stashed my pack down by the docks and the Russians took my rifle."

He nodded and then they followed Joe the rest of the way into town, hunched over and going headfirst into the wind, the snow relentless as it seemed to grow beneath their feet. They reached the end of a long narrow street. There wasn't another person in sight—only squat buildings in various sizes with flat roofs that flanked each side of the narrow lane.

It was a surreal feeling standing on a street that felt as if it were the jumping-off place for the end of the earth. The snowflakes were fast and furious, flying down the narrow lane and heading straight for them as if they were being projected through a wind tunnel. It was terrifyingly beautiful, and he took a moment to just stand and watch nature rage around him.

Eden's hand on his arm had him looking down at her, and he was struck again as he had been the first time he'd looked at her photograph.

He decided it had to be her eyes that made him lose focus. They were big and dark and exotically tilted at the corners. She wore no makeup, but her lashes were long and black and it looked as if she'd lined her eyes with liner, but he knew it was natural.

Her face was paper white because of the cold and her lips void of any color. But still she was the most beautiful woman he'd ever set eyes on.

"Are you all right?" she asked softly and then dropped her hand back to her side.

"I'm fine." He mentally shook himself out of the trance and busied himself looking anywhere but at her. She was dangerous. And she was still an unknown variable as far as the job was concerned. "I just had one of those moments where everything lined up exactly how it was supposed to."

She nodded as if she knew what he was talking about. Maybe she did.

"Those moments are part of the reason I like working alone. When the world comes into sharp focus and you can practically feel the silence living inside of you. Moments like that are rare."

It seemed she knew what he was talking about after all.

"Hey. Chatterboxes. Come, come," Joe said, waving them forward.

The house was right on the corner and didn't seem to be much bigger than an overgrown shoebox. The roof over the wide front porch sagged dangerously beneath the weight of the snow, but Joe didn't seem overly concerned about it collapsing on him.

Navigating the stairs to the front door was a challenge. Nate caught Eden's arm and held her up against his body when she stepped into the empty space between the steps.

He held on to her until she found her footing and he realized at that point that it had been much too long since he'd had a woman that close to him. He'd spent the last few years working almost nonstop, and he was past the age where finding any willing woman was enough. He wasn't a monk, but he'd stopped thinking he could have a normal life outside of the agency. Why was he having those thoughts about Eden Kane?

The siding of the house was bright green, and two square windows not big enough for a body to fit through flanked each side of a peeling wood door. Joe pushed against the door, swollen with age and damp, and they all shuffled into a cozy room with a blazing fire that took up almost the entire wall to their left.

One room was all it was, and Nate figured he could touch both sides if he held his arms straight out. A wood table and two chairs were pushed against the wall and a little kitchenette was set up in the corner.

A woman at least as old as Joe was stirring something that smelled good enough to have Nate's stomach rumbling loudly, and her smile lit up her face as they came in, making Nate think she must have been a very pretty woman in her youth.

She hustled over and spoke to Joe quickly in their native tongue, and then Joe looked to them for introductions.

"This is my wife, Ahnah. She says to hang your coats on the pegs and take these blankets over by the fire and strip out of your clothes. She will wash and dry them for you before your journey."

He shoved two heavy blankets at them and gave them a push. Nate ducked his head to hide his grin at Eden's perplexed look, but she followed him over to the fireplace while Joe and Ahnah huddled in the kitchen area, whispering softly to each other.

Nate unfolded the blanket and saw it was more than large enough to cover him from head to toe, so he wrapped it around his shoulders and then turned his back before stripping out of his clothes and boots. He tried not to think of Eden doing the same. There was no room in either of their lives for entanglements. After everything she'd been through she deserved peace and quiet and comfort. She deserved to be loved.

He wanted to get his hands on Jonah Salt for what he'd done to her, and every time he thought about the level of betrayal it took to pretend to love someone and then shoot them in cold blood, it made him boil with hatred for a man he'd never met. And if Eden didn't kill Salt, then *he* would.

Nate wrapped the blanket so it covered him completely and turned toward the fire. Eden looked completely uncomfortable and out of her element. She was probably thinking being naked was going to be pretty inconvenient if they'd walked into a trap and she needed to start running.

He'd already had the same thought and had made sure he'd palmed his weapons and hidden them beneath the blanket when it had been handed to him. He scooted closer to Eden, so they stood shoulder to shoulder in front of the fire, the wool blankets itchy but warm, and he passed her an extra handgun so Joe and Ahnah couldn't see.

Some of the tension left her shoulders and she looked up at him with a half smile as she hid it quickly beneath her own blanket.

"That obvious, huh?"

"I just figured if I was worried about it, you probably were too."

They stood in uncomfortable silence for a few minutes. He'd never been the kind of man to hold back when he was attracted to a woman. But she was different. She'd been hurt in unimaginable ways, and he realized he'd never put himself in the position of being another person to add to that hurt.

"This would be a really awkward situation if this were a first date," he said to break the silence.

Her eyes got bigger, as if she wasn't quite sure how to respond, but then she said, "I've never actually been on a date, so I wouldn't know."

She'd spoken so softly he wasn't sure he'd heard her correctly, and he froze, unsure of what to say next.

"Never?" he finally asked. "In all the relationships you've had, none of them has taken you out on a date?"

Eden turned those big brown eyes on him and

her mouth quirked a little. "It's not like there's a lot of time for that kind of stuff in this line of work. You don't just slit a Jordanian prince's throat and run off to the movies and share popcorn. There's only work, and the agents who need to satisfy their bodies in more carnal ways establish relationships that suit them best. There's no time for anything in between. And I think it's wasted anyway."

"I'm sorry. Did you just say romance was a waste of time?" Their heads had gotten closer together and their whispers more fervent. "Why do I feel like there's an odd gender reversal going on here?"

"Is that your way of saying you're a woman?" she asked, arching a brow.

Their bodies moved even closer, so his breath whispered across her skin, and he saw by the widening of her eyes that she wasn't completely unaffected by the close contact.

"You want to be careful, sweetheart, about biting off more than you can chew here."

"Did you just call me sweetheart?" Her eyes narrowed, and if he'd been less of a man, in that moment his balls would have shriveled to the size of acorns.

"Don't even try it. You and I both know I

could disarm you before you took aim. Don't play games you don't intend to follow through with."

They'd gone from playful banter to something much more serious in the blink of an eye, and he moved back a step to let things cool down.

"And it just so happens I like going on dates. And I'd have no problem doing my job and then taking you out somewhere afterward."

"Are you asking me out?" The color had drained from her face and she took another step away from him, as if she'd just realized where the conversation was leading. "Oh, no. No, no, no. Definitely not."

"You forgot *non, nein,* and *ne*. Three of my favorite languages."

"My job is to kill Jonah Salt. Nothing else is more important than that. He killed any possible feelings I could ever have for a man again."

"Forever is a long time. It seems shortsighted to think you wouldn't have those desires at some point during the rest of your life."

"If I do, then I'll deal with it. But I promise that part of me is as dead as Jonah is going to be."

"That sounds like a challenge, Agent Kane."

"You're bound and determined for me to shoot you, aren't you?"

He cracked out a laugh and shook his head,

enjoying their short conversation more than he'd expected. A small smile tilted the corner of her lips and he realized she might not trust him—*yet*—but she accepted him as her partner. The other things would come over time.

"Hey," Joe called out. "Chatterboxes. You want to eat?"

Chapter Seven

Eden sat at the little two-person table and huddled over the fish stew Ahnah had ladled into heavy ceramic bowls. Nate sat across from her—she'd stopped trying to figure out how to keep their knees from bumping beneath the table—and she settled in and tried not to think about what that small bit of physical contact made her feel.

Ahnah had gone upstairs to where Eden presumed the bedroom and bathroom were located. At least she hoped they had a bathroom. Walking to an outhouse in this weather would be on par with walking through the fires of hell.

Joe pulled a rocking chair closer to the fire and watched them eat in unnerving silence.

"So how do you know Atticus?" Nate asked. Apparently the silence was getting to him too.

"Oh." Joe shrugged. "We go back. Secret lives and younger days. Atticus's one of the good guys. He tells me you are too, so I help him."

"Did he tell you who we're looking for?"

"Didn't have to." Joe pulled a pipe from the front pocket of his shirt and used the wood of the chair leg to strike his match. He held the flame to the pipe and puffed greedily, his cheeks hollowing as a thin plume of smoke rose from the bowl. He exhaled and a white cloud of pungent smoke filled the room.

"Men come and men go in our corner of the world. And the land eats those who are not strong enough to survive. The man you chase is strong, yes?" The rocker creaked as he went back and forth, the sound almost hypnotic.

Eden's spoon hit the bottom of her bowl and she realized she'd been hungrier than she thought. She was warm and full, and so she settled back against the wall to listen to Joe.

"No offense, Joe." Nate hit the bottom of his own bowl and leaned back against the wall with his arms crossed over his chest. "But if Atticus sent us to you because you're some magical shaman who sees the future in your pipe smoke, I'm going to disappoint you and say we're not interested."

Joe wheezed out a laugh, his rocker coming forward as his feet hit the floor, and he slapped his hand on his thigh. "Boy, there's nothing in this smoke except weed. The medicinal kind," he said, winking. "Helps with my arthritis."

Joe took another puff and started rocking again. "Truth is, my wife is from here and so were my grandparents, but I was actually born and raised in Minnetonka."

"So why the mysterious appearing in the middle of a blizzard in the road routine?" Eden asked.

"It freaks people out, and I find people see exactly what they want to see when they look at me," he said grinning, showing the gaps in his teeth. As if he'd flipped a switch his speech went from the stilted English of a Native to the distinct twang of Minnesota.

Joe's eyes sparkled with laughter and Eden found herself smiling with him. It had been a long while since she'd enjoyed herself quite so much.

"If you didn't want everyone to know you're in town, you shouldn't have questioned Zeke Marley over at the docks. That kid couldn't keep a secret if a gun was held to his head. Everyone in town knows you're looking for a wounded man and that it has something to do with the woman those tourists say was kidnapped this morning. Denny—our chief of police—knows something funny is going on, but there's no proof of anything other than rumor."

"Where would a wounded man go to hide in a storm like this one?"

"That depends on the man." Joe snuffed out his pipe and put it back in his shirt pocket a few seconds before Ahnah came back down the stairs.

Eden guessed by the narrow-eyed gaze Ahnah gave her husband that she didn't particularly care for him smoking in the house. The rapid stream of an obvious scolding left Joe looking a bit like a child who'd just gotten caught with his hand in the cookie jar.

Joe gave a sheepish grin and winked at his wife, while Ahnah scowled and carried two bedrolls over by the fire, rolling them out side by side and leaving a stack of folded quilts and pillows on top. She gave Joe another warning look and disappeared back up the stairs.

"No man would try to brave this storm," Joe continued after she'd left. "It would be foolish, and if you're still hunting this man then he is not a fool. If he is injured, it would be even more of a risk."

"He'd want to stay hidden," Eden said.

"Not difficult to do here. There's a mostly abandoned town at the end of the north road. It used to be filled with those searching for gold, but the gold ran out and the people left. There are lots of empty buildings."

"We've been there," Eden said dryly, thinking of the warehouse and the contraband whales. "We followed his trail as long as we could, but he left the road and it looked as if his tracks continued northwest. The storm was getting worse by that time and we had to turn back. Is there any place in that direction where he could take shelter?"

"Nothing," Joe said, his gray bushy eyebrows rising almost to his hairline. The surprise in his voice made the hair on her arms stand up. "There is nothing but hills and snow. It is not an easy path and there are signs telling all who go in that direction to turn back and go another way. Even in good weather, that path is a death wish."

"Why?" Nate asked.

"Because it's the End of the World. Didn't you research your Alaskan history before you came here?"

"Not well enough, apparently. Why don't you fill us in?"

"It is like the Bermuda Triangle. Only in Alaska. There are places like these all over the world. Where strange phenomena occur that no one can explain. Where a person just vanishes into thin air. Or drops off the face of the planet." He shrugged. "See what I mean? The End of the World. All of those who have set out to find it have never returned. No bodies have ever been recovered. It's as if they ceased to exist the moment they went past the warning signs."

"So you're saying our guy went into the Alaskan Bermuda Triangle?" Nate asked incredulously.

The look on his face was so comical Eden almost laughed. *Almost.* She had a feeling she'd probably pushed him as far as he'd allow for the day. She had to admit it sounded crazy. Maybe Joe had been smoking his pipe too much.

"It's one of the possibilities," Joe said.

"What's the other?" Eden asked.

"That he circled back and is hiding in town the same as you are."

Chapter Eight

Four days of miserable weather pounded the west coast of Alaska, burying it in layer after layer of snow and ice.It had taken Eden less than twenty-four hours for stir-crazy to set in.

The days and nights had blurred into one another—the snow and wind a relentless force. The only difference between day and night was the sky going from a stormy gray to pitch black and back again.

She needed to get out and search for Jonah. The back of her neck had been itching ever since the snow had begun to slow. He was out there. And he was close. He had to be.

Joe and Ahnah's tiny house had one bathroom upstairs with a shower that was so small it was difficult to scrub without knocking elbows against the faucet. But she'd escaped to the small space to put some space between her and Nate, and she let the hot water beat down on her as she tried to think of anything else.

He was driving her crazy, and it hadn't helped that she'd spent each night lying inches away from a man who intrigued her both physically and intellectually.

She'd never met anyone like Nate before. He was an unusual combination of an open book and a man of mystery. Many mysteries. She felt like she'd known him forever and knew nothing about him. Fascinating was the only word that came to mind.

She knew he had a daughter he loved more than anything, and that he'd been divorced for more than a decade. His ex-wife hadn't wanted to live with the secrecy and constant travel, and Nate hadn't blamed her for wanting to move on. They maintained a friendly enough relationship for his daughter's sake, but there'd been no other woman long term in his life.

She knew he liked old black-and-white movies and he hated Chinese food. She knew his sense of humor edged toward the ridiculous and he could make her laugh at the oddest moments. And she knew he slept flat on his back with his gun tucked just under his sleep mat where he could reach it easily.

Just like she knew in her gut that he'd been the agent known as Warlock during his time with the CIA. But she could never get him to confirm or deny her suspicions. He'd been happy to share whatever she wanted to know about his personal life, but his professional life had been completely off limits.

The stories about Atticus's team were legendary. They'd been an unstoppable force and there were contracts out for each of them in multiple countries. She couldn't blame Atticus for going out on his own and setting up shop on a few hundred acres of ranch land in Texas—not answering to anyone he didn't want to answer to, taking only the jobs he wanted to take, and hiring only who he wanted to hire.

Atticus Cameron was a god unto himself, and if the government could get rid of him altogether without starting World War III they'd jump at the chance. Atticus couldn't be bought, he was ruthless, and he was known to always put the people's, and his agents, needs above the puppet masters who tended to run the things of the world.

Those who worked for Atticus were those whose pasts would one day catch up with them if they weren't very careful. Not to mention their families being caught in the crossfire.

She'd missed the dance of getting to know someone. The slow flutters in the stomach and the endless conversations. The last time she'd felt this way was with Jonah, which only served as a reminder that you couldn't trust anyone—not really—and she especially couldn't trust her instincts when it came to men.

But Nate was getting under her skin. A long look from across the table as they played cards or told war stories. A subtle touch against the back of her hand or neck. She knew what he was doing. He was treating her like a skittish horse—easing his way in until she didn't realize how close he'd come. She didn't know how to stop it, but knew she couldn't let it continue.

The problem was she *liked* him. But she didn't trust him. Couldn't allow herself to make that mistake again. She blew out a frustrated breath and wiped droplets from her face. She turned off the water with an annoyed flick of her wrist and grabbed a towel, drying herself off quickly.

She dressed in the clothes Ahnah had washed, and she brushed out her hair, braiding it quickly so it was out of her face. She used the toothbrush that had been given to her and made sure she'd left everything as she'd found it before making her escape.

Eden opened the door and stopped short when she saw Nate standing only a few feet away, a folded towel and change of clothes in his hands.

"Did you have a good shower?" he asked.

She felt heat flood her cheeks and hoped he couldn't read her thoughts. She'd just spent the last fifteen minutes thinking about him.

"You okay?" he asked.

"I'm fine. Just ready to get out of here."

"Joe says we'll have clear skies in the next couple of hours and the weather will stay that way for the next few days."

"Did he see that in his pipe smoke?"

"Nah, he was listening to the weather on the shortwave radio." The corner of Nate's mouth turned up in a half smile. He had a nice smile. It was one of the first things she'd noticed about him. "You're looking a little flushed, Kane. You sure you're okay?"

"Never been better," she lied.

"Then if you don't mind," he said, arching a brow and nodding his head toward the bathroom door. "I think it's my turn now."

The heat in her face flamed hotter and her pulse fluttered just beneath the skin. He was driving her crazy. The sooner they finished this job and got away from each other the better. There was a simple explanation for the attraction. It would happen with anyone she'd been cooped up with for so long. She'd been people-starved over the last three years.

"You can trust me, you know," he said. "You may not believe me, but I'd never do anything to hurt you. Maybe at some point we can figure out a way to help convince you of that."

She didn't turn back to face him. Her pulse was already beating wildly in her throat at the possibility of what he was suggesting. She wasn't so dead that she didn't recognize male interest when she saw it.

Eden escaped while she still had the chance and headed downstairs.

———

Two hours later, the sky cleared just as the weatherman had predicted and the sun glared off the mounds of snow blanketing the area.

It turned out Joe had all of the supplies they needed for their journey. Through the back door of his small house was another building twice the size filled with everything an outdoorsman could possibly want. Apparently, Joe owned the only outdoor supply store along the entire west coast of Alaska. Good business for Joe, and extremely fortuitous for them.

They'd been outfitted in extra winter gear—thermal suits that fit tight against the skin, lined ski pants, a pullover that was too warm unless you were outside in the cold, and down jackets with fur-lined hoods. Water and individually wrapped containers of trail mix and jerky went into their packs along with a first aid kit.

Joe rolled a tent, bedrolls, and a few other provisions into two bundles for each of them to carry on their backs. They weren't traveling light but with the outdoor conditions the way they were, they needed to take every precaution for their survival. The Alaskan wilderness was nothing to toy with.

Joe also had an entire arsenal at the back of his shop for hunters, and she picked up a couple of Glock 9mms—her favorite—and a shoulder holster that fit fairly well beneath the down jacket. She picked up an extra knife for the inside of her boot and noticed Nate's weapon choices were similar to her own. More than likely, any contact they had with Salt would be close contact. They needed him alive so they could get the detonation codes from him.

"I've got something special, just for the two of you," Joe said as he went behind the counter to the locked gun case. "It's a surprise."

"I hate surprises," Eden murmured under her breath, making Nate cough to cover his laugh.

Joe pulled open a drawer and Nate let out a long low whistle. "I'm not even going to ask how you're in possession of these kinds of weapons out here."

Joe just grinned and waved a hand, unconcerned. "You want?" he said, waggling his eyebrows.

"I definitely want," Eden said, reaching for the submachine gun. It had three different settings, so she could shoot one bullet at a time or the whole magazine if she so desired. She hooked it across the bulging pack on her back for easier transport while Nate did the same.

"You ready?" he asked, making a final adjustment of his weapons so he could reach them all easily.

"Yeah. Question is, how are we going to get where we're going?"

"I can help you with that," Joe said. "You know how to ride the sled dogs, yes?"

"No..." she and Nate both said in unison.

"It's either the dogs or cross-country skis. Snowmobiles will run out of fuel before you make it to the End of the World." Joe shrugged. "There is no other way to travel. There are three roads that lead out of Nome, but each of them leads to nowhere. They are literally called the Roads to Nowhere. We are very funny here in Alaska."

Eden pressed her lips together to keep from smiling. She could practically feel Nate's frustration.

"The land is treacherous," he said. "So if you want to get where you're going in a hurry, you take the dogs."

Eden shared a look with Nate and she raised her brows, telling him without speaking that the choice was up to him. It didn't seem like they had any other option, and she saw by the resigned look on his face that he realized it as well.

"I guess we're taking the dogs."

Chapter Nine

Joe had been right. The dogs were a much faster mode of transportation for covering such a large expanse of land. They were also smart and trained well enough to ignore their inexperienced riders. They'd unloaded all of their supplies, except for the guns, into the cargo basket.

It was an eight-dog team, and the moment Eden stepped onto the sled and held on to the driving bar she saw the problem. But it was too late to voice a protest when Nate stepped up behind her, his large body surrounding hers as his hands gripped the handlebars.

The claustrophobia took her completely by surprise. She'd never suffered from it before, but she'd also never been all but swallowed whole by a man like Nate. Her skin turned hot and clammy beneath the layers of her clothes and black spots wavered in front of her eyes.

"Just take a deep breath," he said, his voice soft enough that Joe and Ahnah couldn't hear as they watched to wave them off. "My hands will stay right here." He flexed them around the bar deliberately. "You're in control of the team."

She did as he said and took in a deep breath, the cold stinging her lungs and then coming out in white puffs. Her head cleared and she got control of herself. "I'm fine. I'm ready."

She followed the instructions Joe had given her for starting up the team and they took off like a shot across the snow, pointed in the direction of what Joe called the End of the World.

"Oh, man. My daughter would love this," Nate said into her ear. "I'm going to have to take her to do this on our next vacation."

Eden realized she had a big grin on her face as the snow slushed up around them, the speed of the dogs exhilarating. The sun seemed twice as bright as normal against the white of the landscape, and not even the protective shades she wore could cut the glare completely.

"You do a lot of stuff like this with her?" she asked, settling into the rhythm of the moving sled, adjusting her weight as needed.

"We don't get a lot of time together, so I always make sure we do something memorable. She's a bit of a daredevil and she likes adventures, so it's not always easy finding something that's not completely crazy and still safe for a sixteen-year-old."

"She sounds a lot like you."

"Yeah. It drives her mother crazy."

Eden heard the smile in his voice and turned her head to look up at him, returning the smile. But it faded as she saw how close his face was to her own. She felt the warmth of his breath against her lips. but didn't dare give in to the temptation to glance down and look at them. Instead, her gaze was caught in his dark stare.

It was one of those moments where time seemed to stop as the world continued to rush by around them. She somehow found the strength to turn away, but it had taken more resolve than she'd expected, and she'd had to take a moment to get her racing heart under control.

Nate kept his word and didn't move his hands from the bar, but she couldn't help but notice how the front of his body was pressed against hers. Every jostle and turn had their bodies pressing closer until sweat gathered beneath the layers of her clothes and her body was responding in ways that had nothing to do with the hunt.

What was wrong with her? Nothing had ever come between her and the job before. Not even Jonah. She'd been able to compartmentalize her feelings for him while they were on a mission. But Nate was wreaking havoc with her concentration.

She couldn't seem to control the response of her body. It was chemical—plain and simple. Every mile they traveled became more unbearable.

Fortunately, the dogs helped solve the problem. About halfway to their destination, just past the sign Joe had told them about warning trespassers to turn back or risk death, the dogs pulled up sharp, and if she hadn't had a good grip on the drive bar she would've dumped them both onto the ground. She pressed her foot to the brake, and she had to fight to keep the sled upright, so Nate lent his strength to hold them steady while she called out commands to the dogs.

The sudden silence was unnerving and she slowly released the white-knuckled grip she had on the bar.

"What the hell?" she breathed out in a rush, though she didn't expect an answer.

The dogs moved restlessly, some of them

whimpering as they lay down in the snow, letting her know with certainty that they had no plans to continue on.

She and Nate got off the sled, each of them reaching for the weapons beneath their jackets. They were in the middle of open land in all directions. There were no trees for cover. Just rolling hills of snow. But something had spooked the dogs. Joe had told them they were very intuitive and to pay attention.

They moved into a position where they stood back-to-back, their weapons up and ready for attack if it came. All they could do was listen. But the question was *what* had spooked the dogs? As far as she could tell, there was nothing to make them react as they had.

Silence lay heavy like a blanket with only the occasional rattle of the harness breaking through. There were no fresh tracks in the snow. Nothing but the two of them and wide-open land.

"You want to walk out a little ways?" Nate suggested. "We can circle around, see if we can find what's got the dogs riled."

"Maybe they're not fans of the End of the World," she said, dryly. "Though by my calculations we still have more than a hundred miles to go before we get there."

"At least," he said. "Even with the snowmobile, Salt would've been cutting it close outracing the storm, considering how quickly it moved in."

"Joe said a snowmobile would run out of fuel before reaching our destination," she said. "But knowing Jonah, he's canvassed this terrain dozens of times. This is his playground. He'll have fuel and provisions set up. I'd bet money he's got enough provisions to live on the land for the next year. We'd never see him."

"That would make his attempt at world domination more difficult," Nate said. "He's in prime position for the ultimate power play in being able to control multiple global superpowers through nuclear control. Disappearing right now isn't going to be possible. But you're right about the preparation. He's waiting for us. Let's not make it too easy for him."

Eden did as Nate suggested and moved ahead of the dogs, going clockwise to Nate's counterclockwise until they'd eventually meet in the middle.

Neither of them had elected to wear snowshoes so they could move quickly if they needed to—the snowshoes weren't great for maneuverability and she'd rather take her chances on her own two feet. The downside was the snow came up above her knees, and in some places up to her thighs and hips, as she trudged through.

It turned out the slow movement and depth of the snow was a blessing in disguise. The sound of the trigger as her foot came down was no louder than a click. But it was a sound she'd heard before.

"Oh, God," she said, but the words came out as a strangled whisper. Her muscles froze and the cold sweat of fear raced down her back.

The good news was the land mine didn't automatically detonate as soon as she'd pressed the trigger. But if she took her foot off the mechanism, they'd be finding little pieces of her body in the snow for months.

"Nate," she said as calmly as she could. She held herself steady, one foot keeping the trigger of the land mine pressed down.

He must have recognized the urgency in her voice because he put his gun back in the holster and shuffled in her direction, his feet scooting along the same path she'd already trudged so he didn't end up in the same predicament.

She had to give him credit, he didn't even consider leaving her there to fend for herself and saving himself. He came right to her, despite not knowing how dangerous the situation was.

"I guess we know what the dogs don't like about the area," he said, looking her in the eye with a calm assurance that had her shoulders relaxing a bit. He wasn't going to leave her.

"Let me get a look at what we've got, and then we'll figure out what to do about it. Don't go anywhere."

She choked out a nervous laugh as he knelt by her feet and dug down into the snow, carefully tunneling around the mine.

"There she is," he said.

"So there's gender assigned to land mines?" She stared straight ahead, her gaze locking in on a crag of snow-covered rocks about twenty yards away. Her hands fisted at her sides and she just focused on breathing in and out—for as long as she could.

"I figure anything designed to blow up and hurl shrapnel should be called she. I've been married before, so I remember. I've got a nice scar behind one ear from a perfume bottle that was thrown at my head."

"At least she didn't shoot you."

She felt him pause, so she glanced down to find humor-filled eyes looking back at her. "Did you just make a joke? I think there's hope for you yet, Agent Kane."

"Not if we're both blown to bits while you're taking your sweet time down there. Leave it to a man to make things as complicated as possible."

"It's not me standing on a land mine now, is it?"

Eden couldn't argue with that logic so she just grunted and watched him go back to work.

"He's watching us," she said. "He laid this out. He wouldn't want to miss it."

Nate grunted and stood looking around to see the easiest way for Salt to get a ringside seat to the show. They were surrounded by towering spruce trees, flocked with snow. But sitting on a branch on a tree not more than ten yards away was a small sparrow with red eyes.

"Well, now," Nate said, pulling his Glock and firing off a shot before it had barely cleared the holster. The sparrow sputtered in a *poof* of smoke before it hit the ground. "Hi-tech cameras."

Nate lay down on his stomach so his head touched the snow and looked at it from the side. He moved back to his knees and glanced up at her.

"Looks pretty standard as far as land mines go. I'm going to borrow the knife in your boot. Don't let it freak you out when I touch you."

She nodded and his hand slipped inside her

boot where she'd put her knife. He bent back to the mine and she heard the tiny scrapes as he worked the tip of the knife at the mechanism.

"I just realized it's been a while since I knelt at a woman's feet. And usually she's naked while I'm doing it and not standing on an explosive device. We should try it that way next time."

She choked out another laugh and stared down at the top of his head. His voice didn't betray any of the urgency he must have felt. Mines like the one she was standing on could go off at a moment's notice. And though his voice was level, she saw the sweat beaded on his skin as he continued to work.

Eden felt the knife slide back into her boot and he came to his feet, his body only inches from hers.

"Pick up your foot."

She stared at him for a long moment, knowing she had to trust that he'd taken care of things or they would both end up dead. And then she took a deep breath and prayed.

"Wait a minute—"

Eden froze, her heart pounding as he issued the order, terror coursing through her veins as she waited for the explosion to hit. And then her eyes widened as he leaned in and took her mouth in a kiss that rocked her straight to her soul. Her entire universe exploded into a million pieces.

She hadn't prepared herself for the possibility of his taste—not yet—not when she hadn't guarded herself against the feelings she'd started to develop for him. His tongue slipped past her lips and she heard a moan in the distance—it must have been hers—but the blood rushing in her ears muted her senses so the only thing she was aware of was the man possessing her like he had every right to. It was terrifying. It was exhilarating. And she realized in that moment that she'd never been kissed like Nate was kissing her.

It was just a kiss. But there was nothing simple about it. He invaded her mind and soul and she was helpless to resist him.

Tremors shook her body and her hands came up and gripped his shoulders, holding on as her equilibrium tilted. The heat of him drew her to him like a moth to flame.

It was then she realized both of her feet were suspended in the air, and the mine lay disabled on the ground. She pulled back, her breath coming in short pants and her eyes wide with the shock of whatever had just happened.

"Why'd you do that?" she whispered, though

she didn't think to let go of his shoulders, and he didn't set her feet on the ground.

"I figured if we were going to die we might as well enjoy ourselves on the way out." His breath was just as erratic as hers, and she felt the heat of his fingers through the layers of clothes.

"This is a bad idea, Nate." She pushed against his chest until he stood her back on her feet and then released her. It annoyed her that her legs were just a little unsteady—more so because of the kiss than the threat of the land mine, which was saying something about its potency.

His lips twitched with his normal good humor, but his eyes remained serious. "You have to admit, it was a good kiss. Being naked while doing it would probably be somewhere on the scale of spectacular."

"The last time I was naked with a man, I ended up with three bullets in the chest. You can understand my hesitancy."

"It's a quandary. I'm trying to figure out a way around that so you're not so skittish. I'll let you know when I come up with something."

"Unbelievable," she said, shaking her head, though she had to laugh at his audacity. "You have a skull harder than rock."

"Believe it or not, I've been told that before.

You see this scar here," he said, running his fingers along the side of his scalp. "It's from a bullet. Went right in and bounced off my skull. You and me, Kane. We live charmed lives."

"The thing about that is the charm eventually runs out and you die."

"Which is why we should take life's pleasures where we find them. I've got a little place down in Costa Rica. We should go when this is done. You can wear your bikini."

"Yes, and horrify all the tourists with my scars. I'll pass. Maybe we could worry about finding Salt before you start making vacation plans."

"Okay, but it's a private beach. Your scars don't bother me, so if you wanted to go without the bikini altogether I'd be fine with that too."

"You're exhausting," she said. "Did you not hear what I said about Salt?"

"Oh, I heard," he said. "I was just trying to stall and figure out a way to ask why you didn't bother to tell me that Salt and *Proteus* are one and the same. I don't know why I didn't put it together before now. But it's the only thing that makes sense."

She'd known it wasn't a secret she'd be able to keep forever, and she would've told him. Eventually. When she'd known for sure that she could trust him with that kind of classified information.

"He needs to die," she said instead. "How many agents lost their lives because of him? How many innocent people?"

"You don't have to convince me that he needs to die. But it would've been nice information to have going in all the same."

"Now you know. And our goal is still the same." She moved around him and headed back toward the sled.

"I don't suppose there are any other pertinent facts you need to pass on," he called out. "Now's as good of a time as any."

"You talk in your sleep," she shouted back.

He narrowed his eyes and followed after her, and she turned around before he could see her grin. She wondered how long it would take before he asked her what he'd said, but he remained stubbornly silent.

"We're going to have to go around," he eventually said. "Salt wouldn't have booby-trapped the entire perimeter. It's too much land to cover."

"You realize if we keep going, we'll be walking right into his trap. There's no place for cover around here. He's going to be waiting for us now—watching."

"So we shoot down all his little birds on the way." Nate looked across the great white expanse. "Joe marked a spot on the map where another deserted gold mine is located, but it's at least another fifty miles. It's called Devil's Mining Camp on the map."

"Of course it is," she said.

"Taking the perimeter to the End of the World is exactly what Salt wants us to do. Going off route to Devil's Mining Camp will give us a chance to rest and fuel up. The End of the World will still be waiting for us. If we delay the timetable we'll either piss Salt off, drive him out so he comes hunting us, or—"

"He'll start blowing the targets," she finished.

"That's his plan either way," Nate said. "There's no negotiating at this point. Salt has every intention of blowing those tankers and lighting the world on fire. But he likes the game too much. He's cocky. And he'll want to see this play out. See if we can catch him. See if *you* can catch him."

"And what about the Russians?" she asked.

"One problem at a time," he said. "It'll be dark before we get to Devil's Mining Camp. We've got clear weather for at least a few more hours. That leaves our tracks wide open to anyone wanting to follow. So we need to get moving."

The Russians had been worrying her and she nodded. "It's a chance we're going to have to take. We're the Russian's primary targets. Not Jonah. They see us as the bigger threat. I'm sure they have their own intelligence running interference and looking for the bombs. They don't want us speeding up the explosive timetable if we make a wrong step."

"Just think how helpful it would be if world-wide agencies actually shared information and worked together."

"Well, it is the Russians," she said. "They don't play well with anyone. They'll be out for blood. Ours. And they'll want to make sure we haven't talked. If word gets out that Russian oil tankers are wired with explosives then the trade routes to every country they do business with will be shut down."

"The Russians we can handle," he said. "I'm not so sure about Salt. I know his history at the CIA. He's a legend, but his feats were no more amazing than Atticus and our team. We were all trained by the same person. But Salt being *Proteus* ups the game. He's survived in the darkest parts of underground terrorist organizations for years.

He has contacts we could never fathom. We could use some help in this. Dynamis has a lot of resources. We need to utilize them. There's no reason for you to think you have to take him out alone other than supreme stubbornness on your part."

"Are you trying to irritate me?"

"That's a side benefit," he said, grinning. "How am I doing?"

"You're getting close. And I'm not being stubborn. No one knows Salt and his movements better than I do. I get that all of you were trained by the same person. But Salt trained me. I know how his mind works, his expressions and thought processes. I'm the best bet we have to find him."

"No one is disputing that. But we've found him. He's at the End of the World. Now we just need to kill him. And for that, you're going to need help." He looked at her again and waggled his brows. "How am I doing now? Irritated yet?"

"You've succeeded." She crossed her arms over her chest and arched a brow. "Can we go now or are you going to launch into another diatribe?"

"One day you and I will have a normal conversation."

"I doubt it."

"Maybe over breakfast," he said, ignoring her. "You seem like the kind of person who'd enjoy breakfast conversation."

"I'm going to strangle you in your sleep."

"Strangely enough, you haven't been the first person to tell me that either." Nate checked the compass on his watch and the dogs stood and shook, as if they sensed that he was ready to go.

"I want to find out more about this End of the World and the people who went missing," Nate said, looking at his watch. "Maybe Atticus has some information. And if not, maybe he has an idea of how we can locate Salt and get past his defenses."

Nate got out the bag of dog treats and gave them to the animals, petting one of the lead dogs behind the ears before he came back to the sled.

"You ready to go?" he asked.

The thought of riding for several more hours with her body pressed against him sounded like torture, and from his cocky smile, it looked like he knew exactly how torturous it would be.

"Why don't you take the drive bar this time and I'll ride behind you?"

The smile disappeared from his face and he looked down at her lips before shaking his head and getting onto the sled.

"It's probably for the best," he said soberly. "I guess I can let you hold on to me instead of the handlebar if you're nice. Just don't squeeze too hard. I'm ticklish."

Eden snorted out a laugh and stepped up behind him. "You're a generous soul, Nate. But you're going to regret making the offer." She wrapped her arms around his waist and pressed her body to his back. He sucked in a deep breath and groaned at the touch.

"Maybe I will," he said in a strained voice. "But I've got you right where I want you. I told you I had some ideas on how to get you to trust me. Though you'd think saving you from getting blown into a million pieces would be enough."

"Just mush, Agent Locke," she said, keeping her arms loose in case she needed her weapon quickly. "You make my head spin."

"Well, then. Mission accomplished."

Chapter Ten

Full darkness had fallen by the time they reached the wooden skeleton of the first building of Devil's Mining Camp. There wasn't any reference to the ghost town on the map other than where Joe had circled the *X* he'd made in bright red marker and self-labeled it.

They'd had to take several breaks along the way for the dogs to rest and eat. And once darkness had settled in, they'd had to stop again to put on night-vision goggles. It had been a long and grueling process, and it would be easy for exhaustion to set in, but they had a long journey still in front of them.

Nate put his foot on the brake and stopped the sled. And then he whispered, "This would be a great place for an ambush."

Eden shivered involuntarily. Devil's Mining Camp was perfectly preserved under a layer of white, just as it must have looked a hundred years before. It wouldn't have surprised her at all to see the ghosts of men seeking their fortune walking along the narrow street or saloon girls hanging from the windows, beckoning them to come inside out of the cold and get warm for a price.

She unzipped her jacket and pulled her gun out, holding it down by her thigh. The temperatures had dropped drastically after the sun went down and she flexed her grip around the butt, getting the blood flowing through her hands.

"Creepy," she whispered. She didn't know *why* she was whispering. Only that it seemed like the appropriate thing to do.

"There are no tracks going in that I can see," Nate said, shining the LED light back and forth across the ground. "If anyone's been here, it's been a while. We're going to have to take our chances. The dogs need shelter and rest for the night and so do we."

"Shelter might be overreaching a bit," Eden said as he got the dogs going again. "We'll be lucky if it doesn't come down on top of us."

"It's lasted this long. I figure it can hold another night."

The town began and ended almost faster than a person could blink. It was just one strip of broken-down buildings that sat opposite one another and nothing else. The street down the middle couldn't have been longer than fifty yards and she tried to envision it with horses and wagons making a pass through. A pass through to nowhere. People did crazy things to seek their fortunes and someone had to be the first explorer to find out there was nothing there.

The structures on each end of the street were in the worst shape and provided the least amount of protection, so they opted for one of the buildings in the middle—what had clearly been the saloon. It would at least provide protection from the wind and adequate coverage if anyone tried to sneak up on them.

"I'll take care of the dogs and find shelter for them if you want to make base camp," he told her. "I need to get on the sat phone and get in touch with Atticus." He breathed out a white puff of air and left her alone.

"Strange man," she said as he disappeared from sight. One minute she didn't think he'd ever stop talking and the next he was distant and elusive.

She hefted his pack of supplies over her

shoulder along with her own. She imagined the saloon at one time had swinging doors, but they'd long since fallen down, so only black iron hinges were left hanging from the doorframe. She carefully stepped over the threshold, setting her flashlight on wide beam and shining it slowly across the room.

It was a good-sized area and seemed sturdy enough. There had been wood floors once upon a time, but most of it had rotted, so only the black dirt beneath showed. The rubble of what had probably once been a bar and chairs and tables were scattered throughout, and the staircase that led to the second floor was completely gone, leaving only a gaping hole where it had pulled away from the wall and collapsed in a pile on the ground.

Part of the roof on one side had caved in, so snow had mounded on top of the debris. But she'd camped in worse places, and at least the other half of the room was dry and blocked from the wind. With their insulated gear on they'd be downright warm for the night.

She dumped both packs in the corner and immediately started taking out their weapons so they were ready in case they needed them in a hurry. She found a warped piece of wood that was still fairly sturdy and lined guns and knives up in a straight line along with extra magazines.

Provisions, maps, and the sat phone came out next, and she found a larger piece of wood so she could lay the map out flat. She almost didn't set up the tent, but it was insulated and the added protection against the cold would be nice while they took shifts sleeping. She wasn't sure being confined in such close quarters with Nate was the best of ideas, not after the way his kiss had affected her. But they were both adults, and they could act like it. In the middle of a mission was not the place to get romantically involved. Jonah had taught her that.

Eden looked over at the small arsenal of weapons and grabbed the baby Glock, slipping it into the pocket of her jacket. Just having it close by made her relax a little. Her gut told her Nate Locke was a man she could trust. He'd proven himself by standing next to her while disarming the land mine.

But she was afraid there would always be a part of her that held herself back—waiting and watching—to see if he'd betray her. Acting on physical attraction was one thing. But physical attraction had never been enough for her. Jonah, for all intents and purposes, had been her husband and her first and only lover. And though she realized the farce of it now, she'd thought at the time he'd respected her enough to marry her before trying to take her to bed.

She'd only been attracted to one other—a boy from her childhood. They'd had childish dreams of marrying young and coming to America to start businesses and grow a family, but those dreams had drifted away as they'd both served their two years in the Israeli Army and then she'd been selected to become *Kidon*. That was a life that had no room for dreams and family. But it didn't mean that those dreams weren't buried somewhere deep inside her.

Before she could talk herself out of it she erected the tent and used what materials she could to wedge around the inside perimeter for insulation. Then she laid out the bedrolls, leaving an adequate amount of space between the two. She finished it off by setting one of the flashlights up in the corner so they wouldn't hurt themselves if they needed to get out quickly. The light only gave it a homey, romantic glow, and she debated turning it off but knew that would be foolish.

"There," she said, nodding, as if trying to convince herself she was on a normal op with a normal partner.

"Are you talking to yourself?" Nate said from behind her.

She didn't jump, but it was close. He moved like a wraith. With an unnerving silence for a man of his size and strength.

"We're set up here," she said. "I'm going to take a walk around the perimeter while you talk to Atticus."

"Avoiding isn't winning," he said cheekily. "You know you'll have to talk to him at some point."

She narrowed her eyes. "Last time I checked I haven't actually received a paycheck from Dynamis Security. And to be honest, I'm not all that certain it's where I belong. So until I make that decision, you're the one who can talk to Atticus. I never asked for help on this job. You're the one who elbowed your way in."

He took a step closer and she had to look up to keep eye contact, but she held her ground.

"I would have come for you because that's what my orders were," he said, his smile fading. "But I took one look at your picture and I would've come even if my orders had been to stay as far away from you as possible."

She sneered and her words sounded robotic to her ears. "Just like a man to fall in lust with a face and not think that there might be anything beneath the surface. They must have taken out the other pictures from my file. Believe me, my face is the only thing left of beauty on my entire body, and there's nothing left on the inside except the need for revenge."

Anger flashed in his eyes, but his voice was barely a whisper. "That's where you're wrong. And you don't give either of us enough credit. I recognized something in you the second I saw your picture. You're beautiful, yes. I'm sure you've been told that your whole life. But warriors know how to recognize other warriors. It's in the eyes. There's a depth of knowledge and pain and horror and courage that regular people don't have.

"Those scars on the rest of your body tell a story," he continued. "It tells me you're a woman of resilience and fortitude and unimaginable strength. It tells me you're loyal. It tells me you believe in what you do, no matter the cost. It tells me you have honor and faith. And it tells me that you're the kind of soldier I'd want covering my six. And none of those things have anything to do with the fact that when I look at your face, I'm more than attracted to the whole package."

"Is that all?" she asked, trying to keep her

emotions in check. Her pulse fluttered rapidly beneath her skin and she felt the pressure behind her eyes of tears that wanted to fall.

"I can go on if you want me to," he said, grinning at her in that disarming way he had. She felt the tension leave her shoulders.

"They're just scars, Eden. Nothing more. We all have them. Some are just more visible than others."

She knew he was talking about himself, and the pressure behind her eyes began to burn again, but once again the tears refused to fall. She thanked God for that.

"You've gotten to see the kind of man I am over the last several days. Intense situations bring people closer a lot quicker than normal. You know what else I see in you?"

She was almost afraid to ask and her voice was hoarse when she said, "What?"

"All of those qualities I listed earlier tells me that when you give your heart you give all of it. Which means you must have loved him very much. Which is why the betrayal cut so deep."

She took a shuddering breath and her body started to shiver, but not from the cold.

"He was my husband," she finally managed to say as her teeth started to chatter. "The night he shot me was our wedding night. That's when I found out he was *Proteus*."

Eden was almost comforted by the rage that flashed across Nate's face. It was a secret she'd never told another soul. And deep inside, she knew she could trust him.

"I'm going to check the perimeter," she said, and quickly made her escape.

Chapter Eleven

Nate blew out a slow breath as Eden left him alone.

He didn't know how long he stood there. To say he was shocked was an understatement. There had never been a whisper that Eden and Jonah had been married. Or romantically linked for that matter. Salt had no family at all and was linked to no one. If the agency had known, it would have caused a stir for sure. They tended to frown on interpersonal relationships. Domestic disputes didn't go well while on life and death missions.

He wondered if Atticus had the same rule. In all honesty, he'd never bothered to ask because he'd had no intention of ever getting involved in a long-term relationship again. He already had one daughter who was growing up without her father.

But he was a different man than he'd been back then. Work had always come first.

He'd met Jane riding high after a mission that had almost gone terribly wrong and he and his team had walked into a bar a few miles from the base where she was living in the dorms. She was in the last year of the four she'd committed to serve in the Air Force, and they'd taken one look at each other and never come up for air. There had never been anything but physical between them, but it had been enough for Stella to arrive nine months after that night. He'd gone out on the next mission and hadn't given Jane another thought until he came back a few months later. And boy had that been the shock of a lifetime.

They'd married quickly and quietly and then gone about their respective lives. And luck had been on his side that he'd been between missions when Stella had been born. He and Jane had divorced before Stella's first birthday.

But being with Eden—working with her and fighting beside her—seemed as natural as breathing, and he was starting to have trouble imagining what it might be like without her. He could imagine long-term with her. A life that included shared interests and travel that didn't involve assassinating foreign dignitaries. He *wanted* long-term with her, even if that meant marriage. He knew Eden's upbringing and beliefs were part of who she was. He'd never disrespect that.

Now he just had to figure out a way to convince her that she wanted the same. He could kill Jonah Salt a hundred times over and it still not be enough for what he did to her. Knowing Eden how he did, he understood that shooting her had been nothing compared to the betrayal of her heart.

Before he could dwell on it anymore, he picked up the satellite phone and called Atticus.

"Nate," Atticus answered.

"You've sent me into a complete cluster."

"I sent you to retrieve one agent," Atticus said. "How hard could it be?"

"Almost impossible when it turns out Jonah Salt is alive and she's been hunting him down like a dog for shooting her three times in the chest on their wedding night. Not only that, but Salt has his foot on Russia's neck by wiring up a few of their oil tankers with explosives and blackmailing them for money. And, oh yeah, did I mention that Jonah Salt is *Proteus*?"

There was silence on the other end of the line. And then Atticus said, "Start over from the beginning."

Nate ran through everything that had happened since he'd found Eden in the warehouse, standing over the bodies of Russian intelligence agents.

"What do you need?" Atticus finally asked.

"I need as much information as you can get on an area called the End of the World here in Alaska. Your pal Joe told us that it's an area where people go missing. I think that's where Salt is hiding. And I need Cypher on the tech end of this. I don't want to stumble across any more land mines or something worse. I want satellite imaging and heat-seeking capability."

"Hold on a sec," Atticus said. "Cal is here in the office. I'm putting him on speaker."

Calvin Cruz, also known as Cypher in the hacking community, could work magic with any technology and could build something out of nothing. He was like MacGyver on steroids.

"This is what happens when you send a woman in to do a man's job," Cal said through the speaker. "Heard your lady is putting you through your paces, Warlock."

"You're lucky she's not here right now. She'd slit your throat with the knife she carries in her boot and dance on your corpse. You do not want to go there."

"You always were attracted to the psychos," Cal said. "Let me guess, she's about six feet tall and can pee while standing up. I bet she has a chest hairier than yours. Atticus sure knows how to pick 'em."

"Because I always hire agents based on what they look like instead of skill," Atticus said dryly.

"Hey, I'm just calling it like I see it," Cal said. "All these tough chicks. They'd rather look and act like men instead of using their feminine wiles like God intended."

Nate winced. "Ahh, a true misogynist at heart."

"There's a woman out there somewhere who's going to bring you down a peg one day," Atticus told him. "I hope I get to shake her hand."

Nate laughed. "Are you kidding me? Are you talking about him having an actual long-term relationship with a flesh-and-blood woman? Not One Night Cal," he said, referring to the nickname an old fling had given him. "Besides, his computer might get jealous."

Cal's pride and joy was a computer he'd built and designed for Dynamis. Their relationship just wasn't natural.

"My computer has a name, and she's going to

save your sorry tail," Cal said, offended. "You'd better be nice to her."

"You realize she's not a real person, right?" Nate asked.

"Sure she is," Cal said. "Esmerelda is the perfect woman. She does everything I tell her to do and never argues."

Nate heard the click of a keyboard over the line. Cal was never still or quiet while he worked his magic. The thing about working with the same people for a lot of years and in high-pressure situations was that you got to know them better than your own family. You learned their strengths and weaknesses, the things that set them off or the triggers that could paralyze them at the worst of times.

Just like he knew Cal's attitude toward women was a complete façade to protect himself. He'd lost his wife and both parents in an attack shortly after he'd joined the CIA, and he still blamed himself for not thinking to bury their identities better than just on a cursory level. Cypher had been born not long after that.

Eden came back inside their makeshift campground and he watched her as she dug through her pack for a couple of power bars. She tossed him one and he caught it easily, as well as the bottle of water that followed.

Her face was scrubbed clean and he figured she'd given herself a face full of snow just like he had to wake herself up. The extreme cold was dangerous because it could make a person lethargic, and after the adrenaline rush they'd had when she'd stepped on that land mine, they were both running on fumes.

"That's interesting," Cal said.

"Interesting good or interesting bad?" Nate asked.

"Probably bad. It's going to take some time before I can get you the satellite imaging and heat signals. Someone's trying to reverse the hack and get into bed with my best girl."

"Again," Nate said. "You know she's not real, right?"

"I've tried to pay for therapy," Atticus said.

"Things are about to get nasty," Cal said. "No one messes with what's mine. I know how to treat a lady, and this guy is manhandling my woman. Whatever is at the End of the World, someone doesn't want us to find out about it. We'll just reverse the reverse and I'll give him a little virus. Physical relationships are dangerous these days."

"I'm just going to assume he's talking to the computer," Nate said, rolling his eyes.

"While he's spreading computer-generated STDs," Atticus said, "how are you doing on provisions?"

"We've got about a week's worth."

"That should do it," Atticus said. "Keep the phone close by and give us some time to work it from this end. Stay put for now. I don't want you two walking into a trap."

Nate heard the click in his ear and tossed the phone back on the makeshift table. "Looks like this is our new home for a little while. At least until Cal can get us a satellite image so we can keep going. He's developed this program that can show anything with a pulse in a 3D image as if it were standing right in front of you. It's pretty cool. She'll also be able to do a search and scan for any more land mines or other devices he might have set."

"She?"

"Esmerelda," Nate said. "Cal's computer. He's a bit eccentric."

"Uh-huh," she said.

"Cal's a genius," Nate said. "But don't tell him I said so. His ego doesn't need the boost."

Eden put the power bar wrapper in a sealed

bag and then looked around their living space before finally meeting his gaze. Nate had wondered if she'd get around to looking him in the eye again.

He was about to try to put her at ease when she straightened her spine and opened her mouth to speak.

"I've decided to have sex with you," she said.

He'd chosen that unfortunate moment to take a drink, and he choked on the water, wheezing as it went down wrong. His eyes watered as he tried to suck in a breath and he pounded on his chest while she watched him with an arched brow and a patient look on her face.

"I'm sorry, what did you say?" he asked.

She bent down and started unlacing her boots, and he watched in fascination as she removed a small arsenal from the space. "You don't have to look so shocked. It's not like I'm asking you to commit treason. It's just sex."

"Umm—"

"We obviously have a mutual attraction for each other, but the job has to come first. We should put the physical aspect of this relationship to rest so we can focus on the bigger issues. Besides, the friction and shared body heat will keep us warm."

"Now wait a min—" His mouth went dry as she untied the drawstring on her insulated pants. Who knew a gesture like that could be sexy? He scrubbed his hands over his face and tried to keep his blood in his brain.

"Wait—" He took hold of her hands before she could disrobe any further. "That's all this would be to you?" he asked, surprised at the hurt he felt. She was offering any man's dream. "You're ready for sex after all this time and I'm just supposed to lie down and let you have your way with me?"

"Do you have a problem with that?"

"A little, yeah."

She looked at him curiously, her face a mask to hide her thoughts. "I don't play games, Nate. Not outside of my professional life. Time is too short to try and figure out what other people are feeling and thinking. So I have no choice but to be direct. I haven't wanted another man since Jonah. Haven't even been able to think of a man in that way since then. But I want you. I don't get to choose the time for my body to wake up, or for those beginning feelings of attraction and chemistry and whatever else is going on between us. What else do you want from me?"

"Your trust," he said immediately. "I want to

know that when we're together on an intimate level, it's because you know every part of me at a soul-deep level and you're not waiting for me to plunge a knife in your back. We've got enough complications and distrust in this line of work without adding it to our home life."

"You want me to trust you, but what do I really know about you?" Her hands fisted at her waist. "I've got good instincts, but they've been wrong before. I've got the word of Atticus Cameron—a man I respect and am a little in awe of—who says you're his best agent. Good agent isn't always synonymous with a good person. All I've gotten from you is a glimpse of the man you want me to see. The one who cracks jokes at the wrong time and who watches me with patient and calculating eyes, while looking at me like I'm your last meal."

"Sweetheart, I'm an open book," he said, spreading his arms wide. "What you see is what you get."

He could practically see her teeth grinding together. "Don't call me sweetheart. And if you're such an open book then I should be able to ask you anything I want and get an honest answer. Not a joke or a redirection. Honest. Answer."

"One—" he said, feeling his temper start to rise. "One question only. And then it's my turn."

She hesitated at that, but finally nodded.

"What do you want to know?" he asked.

"Are you Warlock?"

His jaw clenched. "Warlock's dead. And dead men don't walk among the living."

She scoffed. "An open book, huh? And you wonder why I don't trust you."

"That's the problem. You *do* trust me. You're just too much of a coward to acknowledge it."

"That's the first and last time you'll call me a coward."

"Or what?" he asked, his face only a hairsbreadth from hers.

"Or you can explain to your boss why I left you in the middle of Alaska and am giving Dynamis a big middle finger as I go back off the grid. I offered you sex. If you don't want it all you had to do was say no."

"I'm not saying no to sex," he said. "I'm saying no to the kind of sex you want. We've spent the last several days in each other's pockets. I've told you things about myself that not even my team knows. But I'm not here because you're ready to jump back on the sexual merry-go-round. No one wants to be used that way."

"I apologize," she said quickly, and he could tell she meant it. "Really, I'm sorry. I wasn't thinking of it from your perspective. I was trying to deal with my own feelings and I did it poorly. But I don't think I was put on this earth for a relationship. That's an area of my life that's had anything but favor."

"Then I guess I'll be spending the rest of this mission convincing you otherwise. Because wanting you is not the issue. Believe me, I want you. But as much as it surprises me to say, I don't want to scratch an itch with you or get you out of my system so we can focus on the mission. I think after all we've been through we both deserve more than that. Maybe we can achieve it together. And I'd never ask you to compromise who you are and your own personal moral code. And that's exactly what you'd be doing. There's more between us than meets the eye, Eden. There's a future. But I'm a patient man."

Chapter Twelve

Nate took first watch and let Eden sleep.

She'd gotten into her sleeping bag and turned away from him, her Glock in her hand and her knife placed just beneath the corner where she could reach it easily. He'd known sleep hadn't come easily to her and she'd lain awake for a long while, but eventually her breathing had slowed and deepened.

His time alone had given him too much time to think. He'd answered her question truthfully. Warlock was dead. Only his team called him that name, and sparingly. When it did slip it was out of habit. He'd learned to cope with the traumas he'd seen and experienced—the things he'd had to do to others in the name of country. But Nathan Locke and Warlock were no longer the same man.

If Warlock hadn't died then Nate never would've survived. It made it easier to separate the two men—as if Warlock were a figment of his imagination or just a distant dream. Atticus had understood that better than anyone, and he was careful the missions he assigned to Nate for that reason. Bringing back the past wasn't a good idea for any of them.

He knew the second she awoke, even though she lay there for several minutes, listening to her surroundings.

"We're going to have to take the chance and build a fire," he finally said. "The temperature keeps dropping and it's started to snow again. I've got some trail mix if your teeth will stop chattering long enough to chew it."

She sat up slowly and stretched, and he handed her some trail mix and a bottle of water. "A fire would be nice."

"The structure is sound for the most part and there's enough ventilation to let the smoke escape. The floor is dirt, so I could dig a pit and just use some of the scrap wood as a starter. We could move the tent closer and leave the flap open."

"I'll gather the wood and do another circuit around the perimeter," she said.

His mouth quirked as she jumped up and

headed out of the confined space. He guessed she was in a hurry to get away from him.

Being closed up with Nate in such a small space was driving her crazy. She'd picked a heck of a time to notice men again. But not just any man. It was Nate she wanted. She hadn't meant to hurt him, but she could tell her approach to ripping the Band-Aid off in regards to sex, so to speak, had taken him off guard.

It had taken her off guard too. She wasn't the kind of woman who made the first move. She was a slow and deliberate kind of person. And it was because of that reason that she realized it wasn't that she didn't trust Nate. It was that she didn't trust herself.

She'd trusted Jonah enough to not only give him her body, but to make a lifetime commitment to him. What did that say about her?

If she was honest with herself, it was nothing but fear driving her to make such a bold offer to Nate. As if what they'd share wouldn't matter and she could guard her heart. She might not trust herself, but she did know herself. If she was willing to give her body to Nate then her heart was already committed.

The snow and the moon were so bright she didn't need a flashlight to do the perimeter check. As soon as she stepped out of the shelter the wind slapped against her face and icy flurries stung her skin. She pulled up her neck gaiter so it covered the bottom of her face and then went about the business of taking care of her personal needs before she did a perimeter check.

The dogs were quiet and hunkered down out of the wind and snow, and their tracks had already been covered. The weather was inconvenient, but it was also a godsend.

She knew Jonah was out there somewhere, but not even he was crazy enough to attack in weather like this. There was no cover between the moon and the snow, and visibility was low. If the Russians or Jonah had managed to track them this far they'd stand out like beacons and give their positions away.

She found a pile of dry wood that had collapsed under an overhang, and she gathered up the pieces, along with her courage, and went back inside to Nate.

He'd dug a trench in the dirt and found some old pieces of metal that had once been part of a hearth up against the wall. Or what had once been a wall. She stacked the wood onto the metal, leaving plenty of room for ventilation beneath and for the bits of tinder he'd stuffed in his pack from Joe's store. He pushed it beneath the wood and used the survival lighter to start a small flame. It didn't take long for the dry wood to catch and before long there was a nice blaze going.

Eden repositioned the tent as close as it was safe to and opened the flaps wide, but she moved her sleeping bag outside and sat stiffly against a fallen beam to keep watch. The fire crackled and heated the immediate area enough that she took off her gloves and flexed her fingers. Her weapons were within easy grasp and she stared intently at the flames, doing her best to ignore Nate.

"You should get some sleep," Eden said stiffly. "The perimeter is clear, and we're getting a good covering of snow, but dark hours are short in Alaska and it'll be daylight in another hour or so."

"I don't need much sleep," Nate said, settling himself inside the tent on his sleeping bag. He lay down and propped himself up on his arm, not looking the least bit tired.

"What?" she finally asked after several minutes of silence.

"Do you remember the face of the Syrian who tortured you?"

Her breath caught in her chest, and immediately the image of the man who tortured her came to mind. She couldn't have stopped it if she wanted to.

She didn't look at him when she answered. "I see him in my nightmares. His name was Farid. He always insisted that I call him by name. But I never did. I never spoke at all." Her voice was steady as the memories bombarded her.

She could have stayed silent—could've avoided answering Nate's questions like he'd avoided hers. But she wanted him to know all of her—the good, the bad, and the ugly.

"I remember his voice was very soft and gentle," she said. "There was no anger, or hatred or rage. It was a job to him. A job he did very well. There was a look of peace on his face every time he took a hot iron to my ribs. Sometimes I wake up at night and I can still smell my flesh burning."

"It was a job," Nate said, echoing her words.

"We all understand the game we play," she said. "Nothing interferes with the mission. Except death. I killed Farid."

She looked at him then, but there was no

expression on his face. No judgment or condemnation.

"Good," he said. "I can't think of anyone who deserved to die more."

Then he sighed and pushed himself up to a sitting position. She had the feeling he would've gotten up and moved around the room if there'd been more room. She could feel the restless energy coming off him in waves.

"You asked about Warlock earlier," he said.

"Nate," she said, shaking her head. "It's okay. I wasn't thinking. I understand that sometimes secrets are the only way to let something die."

He nodded and his lips pressed tight together. "Warlock was that man. A man like Farid."

Eden froze, but she stayed silent. She could see the rigidness of his muscles, and the veins in his neck as his jaw clenched. As he found the courage to tell her about his past.

"You know how it is," he said. "The government likes to give the media spin about how humane the agencies are. How we don't torture our enemies. About how we only extract information with please and thank you and then let terrorists go on their merry way. But that's all a lie. The mission is always about getting the job done. About protecting this country and the people in it. The agency tells you it's for the greater good. That the secrets we're extracting will save the human race as we know it. It's true for the most part."

"You don't have to explain yourself to me, Nate. I know and understand better than anyone. Our jobs aren't always pretty. But we do them as we see fit because it's never just one person at risk."

"I've stood over the most horrendous, evil men you could possibly imagine. Men without a conscience who killed their own mothers and wives and children to show that they had no weaknesses. Men who bombed schools and hospitals. Power corrupts the mind and soul, and once you get a thirst for it there's no going back. I'm going to put some coffee on."

He rummaged around in the pack and pulled out the small tin pot and supplies, setting everything over the fire. Her mouth watered as the scent of coffee rose. She could tell he was trying to gather his thoughts—determine what to share and what to hold back—and she gave him the space and stayed silent.

"We are the counter to their evil," he said. "But are we really good? I tell myself I am. I know my team is alive to go home to their families because of choices I've made. So I don't regret anything.

"But those choices eventually take a toll on the mind and the body. Especially the job that I had—that Warlock had," he corrected. "There's always a turning point in that particular line of work where you either cross the line and become that person forever—the kind of person who can torture and kill without a second thought. They either end up eating their own bullet because of the terrible things they've done, or they take a step back and decide to walk away from it all. Try to start over. Either way, in life or in death, the horror of it follows. You can never outrun it."

"No, but you can survive it," she said, beginning to understand him a little bit better. "And you were one who was able to walk away."

"Did you know it was our team that was sent in to gather intel on where Osama bin Laden was being hidden?"

"No, but I could've guessed. They'd have sent in the best."

"It was me and Atticus and Cypher. Gabe Brennan had already retired and Damian Huxley was supposedly dead, so our five-man team was already down to three. We each had our jobs. Atticus is like the wind. He blends so seamlessly that you never even realize he's there until it's too late. Cypher worked the tech. And I was the muscle. My job was to get as much information as possible so we could feed it to SEAL Team 6."

Nate didn't mention that the SEAL team was commanded by one of his closest friends. The identities of that particular team were fiercely guarded because of all the high-stakes missions they'd accomplished.

"Timing was crucial, and I did my job exactly how I was supposed to on a high-ranking official of Al Qaida." He held up his hand and flexed it into a fist. "I know just where to hit to cause the most pain without rendering them unconscious. I broke him in eight hours and got all the information we needed. And then I happened to look up in time to catch my reflection in a shard of glass left over from a broken mirror that was hanging on the wall. I didn't even recognize the eyes staring back at me.

"Then I thought of my daughter and wondered what she'd think of her father in that moment. I turned in my resignation as soon as I made it back stateside. Good timing on my part, as Atticus had already been setting up Dynamis and had everything in place. I didn't know it was going to be his last mission too, but he didn't have to try very hard to convince me to join him." Nate let out a long breath as if a weight had been lifted from his chest.

"I'd follow Atticus into hell and back. I *have* followed him into hell and back. And eventually, maybe the good we're doing now will make up for the person I was while working for the CIA. Warlock's death was the best thing that ever happened to me. Until you."

He leaned in and put his hands on each side of her face, causing her breath to catch, and he kissed her on the lips gently before releasing her.

"You can't tell me you don't feel it too," he said. "We live a life that's fast and furious. We're trained to assess people and situations and feelings quickly. You and I are people who know what we know and make life and death decisions in seconds. Because our life depends on it. And I'm telling you what I know—that you and I are two missing pieces of a whole. Everything we've done and experienced up to this point has led us to where we are right now."

"And where are we?" she asked.

"We're together," he said.

Eden realized in that moment that the feelings she'd had for Jonah would have burned off eventually. They were too hot and bright. But she saw a steadiness in Nate. A promise of stability. A promise of a lifetime. And that was something she hadn't thought she'd ever want again. Growing old in their line of work wasn't typical. But if she let herself imagine, she could see herself growing old with Nate. She could love him. And if they made it out of this mess alive, she promised herself she would tell him.

Chapter Thirteen

The snow was relentless for the forty-eight hours, but the backs of both of their necks were itching and a restlessness had settled over their camp.

"I know Atticus wants us to stay put," Nate said, rubbing his hand over his eyes. "But my gut is saying that we need to get out of here. The snow is still coming down, but it's not harsh and the sun will rise soon. I'm too old for this. I miss my bed."

He'd just woken from a couple of hours of sleep while she'd kept watch, and her lips twitched at his grumpiness.

"My gut is in the same place yours is," she said. "We've got time to refuel and pack up before we head out."

He grunted and said, "I'll do a perimeter

check and then call Atticus and let him know there will be a change of plans. Maybe you could make more coffee."

She hid her smile and built up the fire. Nate was a cheerful and good-humored guy for the most part, and Eden appreciated that he could go from relaxed to business in the blink of an eye, but she'd learned that coffee definitely helped keep him at his best. Morning was not his best time.

Once she got the coffee going she got up and stretched before making her own perimeter sweep. There was nothing but white in all directions for miles. And there was nothing but silence. It truly felt like the end of the world. But there was something lurking—something waiting. She could feel it on the back of her neck. And she'd learned never to ignore those feelings. Nate was right. They needed to get out of there.

She went back inside the abandoned saloon, noticing Nate had already returned and was helping himself to the coffee. He handed her a small tin cup filled with black liquid and closed his eyes with pleasure as he took his first sip.

"It's nice to know you have a weakness," she said. "Do you lose all your spy superpowers if your caffeine levels get too low?"

"Look at you making a joke," he said. "I'm so proud. I've been told I'm a bad influence."

Her mouth twitched, but she didn't let herself smile all the way. Old habits were hard to break.

"It's all clear out there," she said. "There's nothing for miles. And no tracks but ours. The dogs are calm and don't seem disturbed. But—"

"Yeah, I know," Nate said.

She rolled the knots from her shoulders. "The only question is where are we going from here? The End of the World is the trap Jonah set up for us. I can't imagine there's too many places for cover along the way." She sighed. "I hate the snow. We should have brought more firepower."

Nate stood in front of the table where she'd laid out all their weapons. They were each carrying their personal pieces, but there were backups, plenty of magazines, a couple of hand grenades, and the two H&K MP5 submachine guns.

She'd stripped out of her heavy coat, leaving her only in the black ski pants and the matching thermal top. She braided her hair and pulled a black watch cap low over her ears. Nate was dressed identically to her. Neither of them wanted to have to fight with the weight of extra clothing if they needed to move quickly.

"Jonah is a ghost," she said. "Obviously. Wide-open territory isn't going to faze him. And if he can get the Russians to take us out for him more's the better. We're right where he wants us to be. He's lasted as *Proteus* for as long as he has for a reason."

The sat phone buzzed against the warped wooden table and Nate hit the button so it was on speaker.

Atticus's voice filled the room. "You've got incoming heat, and they're moving fast. Cyph was finally able to get the satellite imaging up and running."

"Not my fault, man," Cal said. "I had to hack into NASA and the Pentagon to get them, but I'm your eyes now."

"It looks like you've got a six-man team bearing down. They're about five kilometers out," Atticus said.

"Nothing like short notice," Nate said. "They're practically right on top of us." Nate pulled the strap of the MP5 over his shoulder and let it hang in front of him. "Better to take them out here than in the middle of nowhere with nothing but spruce trees for cover."

Eden grabbed extra magazines from the table and took the other MP5, though she didn't bother with the strap because it would only get in her way.

"We can use the area to our advantage," Nate said. "We've been here long enough to get acclimated."

"We need to split up," she said, knowing how his mind worked well enough to guess the game plan. "One of the buildings across the street has good coverage. I'll take point there."

Nate pocketed the two grenades and checked the magazine in his Glock, putting it in his pocket when he saw it was only half full. He grabbed another and popped it in, chambering a bullet.

"I'm going to set the dogs loose. Joe said they were trained to find their way home. I don't want them caught here."

Adrenaline pumped through her system with the force of a thousand men. The dogs were their only transportation. Without them they were going to have a hell of a time tracking down Salt. But there wasn't time to argue, and she knew he was right, so she nodded and took off out the front door to the building she'd marked on the opposite side of the street.

Nate released the dogs and gave them the command Joe had told him to send them home, and he barely made it back under cover before he heard the low buzz of engines in the distance.

"Keep the link open," Atticus demanded. "We can see their shoe size from here and they're packing major heat."

Nate could tell as soon as the first snowmobile appeared at the edge of town that these were a different caliber of Russian agents than the ones who had held Eden in the warehouse. He watched in silence through a rotted hole in the wall, and then swore as two of the agents peeled off and went behind the buildings.

The good news was that everything was in close quarters. He could throw a rock and hit one of the buildings across the street. The lane between the two sides was narrow, and the Russians would be sitting ducks if they came down that way.

"Oh, hell," he whispered as one of the agents hefted a rocket launcher and settled it on his shoulder.

The Russian didn't know where he and Eden were hiding, but that didn't matter. His goal was to smoke them out, get them out in the open. And it was a pretty effective way of doing so.

Before the man could get a shot off, Nate moved outside of the building and pulled the pin on the grenade in his hand, launching it toward the enemy. He'd just given away his position, but it was sure as hell better to take the offensive than having to dodge rockets.

The four agents scattered like bowling pins as soon as they saw the grenade, and the explosion rattled the fragile building that was his only protection. Gunfire erupted and he knew without looking that Eden had the sub on full auto and was laying down cover so the Russian with the rocket launcher couldn't get that shot off.

"You've got two heat signals coming from the opposite end of town," Cypher said through the phone.

As long as Eden kept laying down cover, he could take care of the others coming in. He caught them by surprise, moving quickly so he was almost perpendicular with them when he took them down. Two quick rounds to the chest and the enemy was now four instead of six.

The Russians were returning Eden's fire now, having found their own places for cover, and he made his way back up the strip. A man stepped out in front of him, so close there wasn't room to get his gun up in time, and he barely ducked back as the blade of a knife swiped toward his middle.

He didn't feel the cut along his side, but he smelled the blood. Nate grabbed the man's wrist and twisted, hearing the satisfying crunch of bone as his fingers went limp and the knife dropped to the ground. Another punch to the throat killed the man instantly. He kept moving forward, toward Eden.

A body lay prone in the middle of the lane, the snow beneath him bright crimson. But Nate's blood turned cold and his heart stopped in his chest when he heard Eden's yell and the sound of the rocket launcher as it fired straight at the building she was using for cover.

He started running. And praying. And he watched with amazement as Eden's body shot out of the building just before the rocket hit, curling up in a ball at the last minute so she rolled out into the middle of the lane as the building exploded behind her.

The two remaining agents stepped out of their hiding places, their weapons trained on her, and all he could think was that he couldn't lose her. Not like this.

He sprinted to the bigger of the two men and knocked the gun up just as he was about to fire, so the bullet went wild into the sky. This agent was better at hand-to-hand than the other, and didn't let Nate get in too close. They were evenly matched and it was only hearing similar sounds of combat coming from Eden and the other agent that had him taking a chance to reach into his boot and pull the knife, striking it between the man's ribs and into his heart before he could deliver his own killing blow.

Eden couldn't show weakness. Couldn't let her guard down. Blood dripped into her eye from the cut above her eyebrow and she wiped at it quickly as she dodged a punch from the man who'd fired the rocket launcher.

She knew how to fight. Knew that concentration and focus was the most important thing. But something broke through that concentration, and before she could blink the man had her in a headlock, her breath cut off and her lungs burning. Blood rushed in her ears, muting the sounds around her, but she realized with complete clarity what had broken through her focus.

It wasn't the static of the sat phone from somewhere in the distance and Atticus's frantic warnings. But the pitched tune of "Pop Goes the Weasel" being whistled in a rather upbeat tempo.

It was that moment she knew she was going to die—the arm around her throat was cutting off the oxygen to her brain, but it was Jonah Salt whistling from just over the hill who would deliver the killing blow.

The man holding her captive jerked behind her and his arm loosened around her throat, so she was able to greedily suck in air. The report of a rifle had been close and she managed to get a glimpse of the man who'd held her, a neat bullet hole right in the center of his forehead.

"Down," Nate yelled. But her brain and her reaction time were slow. She felt his body jerk as he knocked her to the ground, his body covering hers as the sound of another shot being fired penetrated the fog in her brain.

"Get up! Get up!" She knew he'd been hit, but he had her up on her feet, his body hunched over hers for protection as he ushered her back toward the safety of the buildings.

Chapter Fourteen

"What the hell was that?" Atticus said through the open line once they made it back to home base. "I've got six bodies on the ground and then a heat signal comes out of nowhere and starts laying down rifle fire."

"It was Salt." Eden's voice was barely discernable and Nate handed her a bottle of water. "I heard him."

"I'm sorry, what?" Atticus asked.

"He whistles while he works. He always has. The sound of it broke my concentration and that Russian agent almost snapped my neck."

"And then Salt shot him and saved you?" Cal asked. "That makes no sense."

"It's part of the game," Nate said, looking at her intently. "He wanted her to know he was there. That he was the one pulling the trigger. He killed the immediate threat so she'd know."

"That is messed up," Cal said. "But I've got his heat signature now. I'm following him back to wherever he was hiding. And he's moving at a fast clip. He's got a snowmobile. I'll be able to find his hiding place and then you'll have the coordinates you need to flush him out."

"You guys okay?" Atticus asked.

Eden looked at the blood that covered Nate's arm and stomach, but he shook his head no at her, telling her not to mention it to Atticus. He dug around in their supplies and came out with the first aid kit and then stripped off his shirt.

"We're fine," Nate said. "Nothing we can't patch up with the first aid kit."

Eden raised her eyebrows at that statement, thinking it might be a little overzealous. She moved closer and took the kit from his hands and then pointed with her finger, telling him to sit without words.

He leaned in and kissed her softly on the lips, and then pulled back to look at the cut over her eye.

"It's fine," she whispered. "But you're going to need stitches."

He grunted and sat down where she pointed

while she went about gathering the supplies she needed—fresh water and wood for a new fire.

"What the hell?" Cal said, after a few minutes of silence. "No, no, no. This can't be possible."

Dread knotted in Eden's stomach as the rapid click of the keyboard was heard across the line, and Cal's unintelligible mutters were interspersed with a lot of interesting curses.

"He's gone," Atticus said.

"What do you mean gone?" Nate asked. "He can't just disappear."

"And yet, that's exactly what it looks like from where we're standing. I was prepared for something like this."

"Maybe you should fill me in, boss, because I'm confused," Nate growled out. "Why would you expect him to disappear into nothing? Unless you believe all the legends about this being the end of the world. Did he just drop off the planet?"

"Close enough," Atticus said. "I did some digging, and that particular area was once an underground KGB headquarters. It was completely off the books and functional up until 1991 when the KGB disbanded. That coincides with the timeline of the last couple who disappeared from that area—a man and woman who were self-proclaimed adventurers. More than likely they got too close and were captured. The KGB would have made their bodies disappear for good."

"Lovely." Nate scrubbed a hand over his face and it came away with dirt and blood.

"Are the two of you secure for now?" Atticus asked.

"Unless Salt decides to come back and play some more."

"Good. Give us a couple of hours to dig out some more information. We're close. Really close to getting a lock on all of this. Stand by."

The phone disconnected and Eden reached over and hit the off button. "I'm sorry I dragged all of you into this."

"Honestly, I can't think of anywhere else I'd rather be," he said, lips quirking. "It's no Hawaii vacation, but it's had its perks. I'm just glad I found you when I did. You couldn't have continued to go after him alone. Not without getting yourself killed."

"No, but I would've kept going because the revenge was all I could see."

"And now?" he asked.

She smiled and knelt down by the fire, lighting the tinder and listening to the wood crackle a moment before she answered him. "And now things are a little clearer. I'm grateful for the help. You're a good partner."

"You're not so bad yourself, Kane. Partners... I like the sound of that. I can't think of anyone else I'd want to watch my back for the rest of my life. Or scrub it from time to time."

Her hands froze inside the first aid box and she didn't have the courage to look up at his face to see what he meant by that statement. Instead she relaxed and pulled out bandages and a needle and thread.

"If I'm destined with working in the field for the rest of my life, I give you permission to go ahead and put a bullet in my head. The body can only take so much wear and tear. Our days in the field are numbered. There's always someone younger and faster and more clever to come along. And like you said, it's nice to go home to a soft bed."

She'd put the bottles of water next to the fire, hoping it would warm them some, but it wasn't going to be warm enough.

"Nah," he said, grinning. "There's a lot to be said for age and wisdom. Present mission excluded, I've managed to get in and out of most jobs without fighting or getting shot. Wisdom is really a nice thing to have."

Her mouth quirked. "I guess I'm not old enough to have any of that yet. I must have a few years left in me yet. Grandpa."

He arched a brow. "Remember how I told you I've got this great little place down in Costa Rica? With a private beach and a view unlike any other. I bought it more than a decade ago with the idea it's where I'd end up after I retire. The sad thing is I've been there three times in ten years. Let me know the second you start thinking about retirement and I'll buy the plane tickets."

"I don't think people like us do well in retirement," she said. "Sitting still and doing nothing isn't one of my strong suits."

"Maybe we don't go for retirement," he said. "Maybe we go for a honeymoon."

The heat in his eyes was so intense she forgot she was supposed to be tending to his wounds.

"One step at a time," she whispered, blowing out a breath. "This is going to be cold." She grabbed one of the water bottles and a clean cloth. The wound on his arm and across his stomach had to be cleaned before she could sew him back up.

"I've had worse," he shrugged. "Just get it done. Let me ask you a question."

"Whatever you need to do to distract yourself," she said.

"Do you want me?" He hissed out a breath as the frigid water ran over his wounds. "Like, physically? Are you attracted to me in that way?"

The vulnerability in his voice surprised her. She couldn't imagine a man like him had ever been unsure of his attractiveness to the opposite sex.

"Not at the moment," she said, narrowing her eyes in concentration. "Seems like bad form to take advantage of a man in your current state."

"Very funny," he said. "But seriously. All cards on the table. You're it for me, Eden. I knew it the moment I saw your picture in the file. I can't explain it. Maybe it's supernatural. Maybe it's fate. I don't know, and I don't want to think about it too hard because my head is starting to hurt. I just need to know that you feel something."

"I feel something," she said, cleaning the areas as thoroughly as she could. "You know I do. I feel more than I ever thought I'd feel again. Which scares the hell out of me. I want you. The physical is there. But I also like you, even though you drive me crazy sometimes. And I think I could choose to love you."

"Choose to love me?" he asked.

"The bullet passed through," she said. "That's a stroke of luck. I'm not great at digging bullets out of people."

He growled and she smiled, threading a needle so she could stitch him up. The cut along his stomach was long and red, but it would be fine with butterfly bandages and antiseptic.

"Love is not an emotion," she said, making the first stitch. "It's a choice. Maybe that takes the romance out of it for some people, but to me the choice makes it all the more romantic. Choosing to love someone day in and day out is the hard part. Emotions are easy. The flutters in the stomach and the euphoria of new love—getting to know someone to their very core. Sex.

"But those things fade over time. Choosing to love someone takes effort. Every single day. Choosing to stay through the different stages of life—children, sickness, death of loved ones, career changes, hormones—that's when you really understand what love is. If I choose to love someone, I mean it. I don't make promises lightly."

She finished stitching him up and wrapped a

bandage around his arm, and then she pulled back to see his face.

"Thanks for pushing me down," she said. "You saved my life."

She touched her throat and it was tender to the touch from where the man's arm had pressed against her, cutting off her oxygen. It was swollen and getting harder for her to speak. But only time and rest would heal it.

"I knew the second the bullet was fired and hit the man holding me that there'd be another one for me," she said. "I should have known Jonah would want a ringside seat to our deaths. Just to make sure we were out of his way and he could move on with his plan. But I've been his only failure. He didn't kill me that night in France. And he wouldn't have wanted to give anyone else the pleasure. I really thought that was the end for me. I was waiting for it."

Eden took a long drink of cold water, hoping that would soothe the burn. Nate's hand came up and cupped her cheek gently and she leaned against it.

"It's never over until you give up." He brought his lips to hers—softly—soothing. It wasn't a kiss of high passion. This was an easing into each other—an acceptance. He pulled back and smiled. "I wasn't ready to give up yet. Not when I've just chosen you."

She nodded because that's all she could do, and then she went about the task of patching up the wound across his stomach. It didn't take long, but by the time she was finished, sweat had beaded on Nate's brow and he was shivering from the cold.

"Get some clean clothes on and get warm," she told him.

"I will if you'll let me take care of that cut above your eyebrow. You'll keep opening it up and bleeding if I don't close it."

She nodded in agreement and passed over the supplies. His hands were gentle as he put butterfly bandages across the cut.

"I've got a confession to make," he said once he was finished. His fingers trailed down her jaw and glanced over the line of bruises across her neck, and she watched his face darken with anger.

"What's that?" Her voice cracked under the strain.

He met her gaze and the heat there almost knocked her over with its intensity. "Watching you dive out of the front of that building as it exploded was one of the sexiest things I've seen in my entire life. If we weren't both injured right now I wouldn't be opposed to starting our wedding night early."

"Wedding night?" she said, all color draining from her face. "I don't have such a good track record with those."

"I just wanted to say it out loud so you can get used to the idea. No rush. All in your timing. Or if we survive this. Whichever comes first."

Eden felt like she'd just taken a cannonball to the stomach. Fortunately she didn't have to think about it too hard because the sat phone started buzzing again.

Chapter Fifteen

"It's time to lock and load," Cal said excitedly on the other end of the line. "I cracked her wide open. This is the moment where you all should be congratulating me."

"Why don't you tell us what you did first and then I'll send you a fruit basket," Nate said.

"Why do you want me to explain? You won't understand any of it anyway."

"You and I are due a round in the ring, my friend."

"Bring it on, buttercup," Cal said. "I've got youth on my side."

Nate rolled his eyes. "You're only two years younger than I am. You're not exactly the picture of youth."

"I'll take whatever advantage I can get. Your fists are like ham hocks. Hurts like a—"

"I'm sorry," Eden interrupted. "But you were talking about cracking her wide open, whoever *her* is. Maybe you could expound on that a bit. Don't get me wrong, we haven't met in person or anything, but I'm starting to think you might deserve that ham hock to the face."

There was surprised laughter from Atticus and Nate. She was starting to feel like she'd fit right in at Dynamis Security.

"I think I'm going to love you, Agent Kane," Cal said. "Now listen close, because we're going to be working on a time clock here. I've got complete schematics of the former KGB base. We're talking a lead-lined bunker that goes into the ground almost fifty feet. That's why Salt disappeared off the map. Once he goes underground there's no heat signature.

"Salt has set up the ancient KGB computer system to piggyback off the CIA's mainframe. It's actually an ingenious way to go undetected because the technology is so old. My guess is he's been there for a long time. This is *Proteus*'s headquarters. He can keep a close eye on the devices he's planted across the globe, and he's got the detonation switch at the tip of his fingers. Every time one of these bombs detonates it'll be traced back to US soil. He's on the precipice of starting World War III and setting himself up to become the supreme ruler once all the dust and bodies are cleared."

"So how do we keep him from blowing the tankers?" Nate asked. "I'm assuming he'll know the moment we get near to his base. He has to have infrared technology in a place like that. Not to mention he's got outside camera coverage. We've already found one of those."

"I've got you covered," Cal said. "I was able to piggyback off his piggyback, if that makes any sense. I'm running the shots as long as I'm tapped in. But here's the problem. The detonators are set to explode automatically if he doesn't log in and type in a password every six hours. It's a failsafe in case something happens to him."

"Lovely," Eden said with a sigh. "Nothing is ever easy."

"If it was we wouldn't be making the big bucks," Cal said.

"Again, still not on the payroll," Eden said.

"To be fair, you kickstarted this mission," Cal said. "I'd much rather be preparing for my fantasy baseball draft."

"Getting back on point," Atticus said.

"Yeah, yeah," Cal said. "I can shut down Salt's sensors without him knowing before you get into range, but I'm close to being able to reprogram the detonation codes so the ones he does have will become inactive. I've programmed the route he took into your watches. It's not far. You'll be able to make it on the snowmobiles of your dead Russian friends. I'll follow your progress from here."

"So we're basically walking into the lion's den without knowing how to get through the doors?" Nate asked.

"I'm still working on that part," Cal said. "All you've got to do is capture Salt. Let me worry about disarming the tankers. Just get moving. By my estimation, he's got a little over an hour before he needs to check in and type in the codes. Do you guys have comm units? The sat phone won't be viable once you cross a certain point."

"Yeah," Nate said. "Joe set us up. It must be nice to be sitting behind a computer screen a couple thousand miles away right now."

"I'm not complaining," Cal said.

"Don't worry," Atticus cut in. "He's up in the rotation for the next assignment."

"It'll probably be guarding some heiress in a

five-star hotel somewhere," Nate said. "Bastard has all the luck."

"You know how much I hate the cold," Cal said deadpan. "Kane's lucky she got you for this round."

"I'd say so," Eden chimed in. "I would've put a bullet in you by now."

Nate barked out a laugh and watched the smile tug at Eden's lips. "Signing out and turning comm units on. Watch our backs out there. He's not going to play nice."

"Roger that."

Eden checked her watch as it beeped and coordinates began coming through, and then she took the earpiece Nate handed her and put it in her ear, closing her hand over it so no one could hear.

"Cal said we're supposed to capture Salt," she said. "I'm not doing that. I *can't* do that. He has to die."

"I'm not going to tell you what you should do," Nate said. "That's a choice you'll have to make. But I'll have your back either way."

She nodded and put in the earpiece.

"Checking in with control," Nate said, once his own was in place.

"Reading you loud and clear," Cal said. "You

guys keep the sexy talk to a minimum. Though I've got to be transparent, Kane. I've got twenty bucks riding on whether or not you shoot him down if Nate makes a move. I heard he was quite entranced by your picture. It's not often our boy strikes out at the plate. I wish I could be there in person to collect my winnings."

"You're going to lose that bet," Eden said. "We're already talking marriage. We're honeymooning in Costa Rica."

Cal snorted and said, "Good one," obviously thinking she was joking.

They collected weapons and checked ammo, and put on their heavy jackets and hats for the ride.

"Our Russian friends had excellent taste in transportation," she said, eyeing the snowmobiles at the end of the street. "These even have heated seats."

"I think they'd want us to have them," Nate said, spinning the MR5 around so it hung on his back. "There's no snow in hell. You ready?"

She nodded and straddled the red snowmobile, turning the key and listening to the engine purr. There was plenty of fuel, and she made sure her weapons were adjusted for easy access. Nate did the same and gave her a thumbs-up as he pressed down the accelerator and they left Devil's Mining Camp.

"I'm going to miss that place," he said. "It was starting to grow on me. Maybe we should honeymoon here. We could probably buy the whole town."

"You're a laugh a minute," she said. "Look at these tracks. Jonah has been circling us, probably since the time we arrived. If the End of the World is close by he would've been able to bunker down when the weather hit. Always a step ahead."

"This is his territory," Nate said. "What he's not expecting is someone like Cal about to ruin all his plans."

"That's me," Cal said in their earpieces. "Ruiner of plans. Just ask my mother almost every holiday."

They used the coordinates on their watches to keep on course, and the watch buzzed as soon as they hit the perimeter of their destination. They brought the snowmobiles to a stop and Eden looked around in all directions.

"We've got a small problem here, Cyph," Nate said. "We're at the end of our destination and there is nothing here but snow. A lot of snow. Mounds of snow. There are snowmobile tracks all across and back again, but there's no sign of any kind of structure."

"That's the tricky part," Cal said. "You're standing right on top of it. Now we just have to figure out how to get you in."

"You don't know how?" Nate asked incredulously.

"I'm working on it. You guys always expect the impossible, and nothing is ever that easy."

"My apologies," Nate said. "Just take your time while we stand here and twiddle our thumbs."

"I do have good news," Cal said. "I broke the codes for his antipersonnel explosives so the ones he has are no longer operable. Atticus is making the call to the SEALs so they can locate the ships and remove the devices. So all you have to do is make the capture. Atticus wants me to remind you to bring him in alive if possible. The CIA has gotten word somehow that Salt is in the wind. We think your Russian intelligence boys tipped them off to complicate things."

"We'll deal with it when it comes to that," Nate said, reaching over to squeeze Eden's hand, but she was like a statue and he could see the pain on her face. "You've got to have some idea how to get inside this building. The snow is piled in an unusual pattern, almost a spiral shape, but I'm still not seeing a door or any signs of concrete or metal. I'm afraid to take the snowmobiles too close."

"Leave them where you are and go by foot," Cal said. "Maybe you'll trigger something."

"I triggered a land mine not too long ago," Eden said. "I'd prefer not to do that again."

"I meant a keypad or some kind of activation pad for entry. Geez you guys are way too serious."

Nate rolled his eyes and they dismounted from the snowmobiles, each of them holding their Glocks down by their sides. As they moved closer to the coordinates on their watches the vibrating on their wrists increased. The snow was deeper in some areas than others, but the ground was different here.

"We're right on top of it," Eden said. "We can't get any closer."

"There's some type of voice activation code, but it's not anything I recognize," Cal said. "It's not a voice command. The frequency is wrong. But it's some kind of sound. It's a high frequency and pitch. I'm filtering it through the system now to see if I can come up with a match."

"You think it's electronic?" Nate asked.

"That could be a possibility," Cal said.

"No," Eden said. "It won't be electronic."

And then she started to whistle. "Pop Goes the Weasel." Just like Salt had whistled before shooting at her earlier. It was another part of his game.

The ground trembled beneath their feet and the snow shifted as stairs that led into the earth seemed to appear from nowhere. Eden and Nate both moved back out of the way and spread out from each other, trying to keep their balance as the ground continued to shake.

She heard the answering whistle as Salt appeared at the top of the stairs, and she raised her gun.

"I wondered if you'd figure it out," he said, his smile sending chills down her spine. He ignored Nate completely. His eyes were only for her. "You were always a bright student. Hard to kill. But very bright."

"Jonah Salt," Eden said. "You're to be transported to Langley on charges of treason and terrorism."

"No, I don't think so. You forget the little matter of the oil tankers that are set to blow. In fact," he said, checking his watch, "if I don't type in the codes to disarm them in the next eight minutes... Boom." He spread his hands in a gesture to indicate an explosion. "It'll be bad, love. It's best if you and your friend find a safe place to hide."

Salt finally looked over at Nate and his smile faded. "Oh, wait. Never mind. I've decided to kill you instead. Six feet under is as safe a place as any, I guess."

Nate let Eden do the talking. The connection between the two of them was obvious, and he didn't want to set Salt off by interrupting.

"I've got bad news for you, Jonah. Your little devices have been deactivated. It turns out you're not quite as good at covering your tracks as you think you are."

"Don't con me, Eden. There are less than a handful of people who could decipher those codes to deactivate the entire system."

"Good thing one of those people is on our team," she said. "But if you don't want to believe me that's fine. We can stand here for the next six and a half minutes and see what happens when you don't check in. I've got nowhere to be at the moment."

Cal hissed through the earpiece. "Are you crazy? Don't antagonize him."

Salt stared Eden down, trying to decide if she was bluffing or not, and he finally sent her a knowing smile that had ice forming in Nate's gut.

"So we're at an impasse, it seems," he said. The corners of his mouth quirked and his eyes were stone cold. "I have other projects, though this one has been very lucrative so far. Ruling the world comes with its setbacks from time to time. And I've been ruling the world for a while now. If I'd known how tenacious you were going to be, love, I might have brought you in on it. You did have—" he looked her up and down with a sneer on his face, "—certain attributes that I found very enjoyable. Oh, by the way, is this a bad time to tell you I want a divorce?"

It took everything Nate had not to give in to the temptation and unload his weapon into the pompous jerk. His arm jerked in reflex, but he kept the gun down by his side. But it was enough movement for Salt to notice.

"Ahh, that bothers you does it, Agent Locke? Our Eden likes to spread her favors around, so it seems."

Nate let the rage rush through him only to be replaced by ice. There was no use for anger in a volatile situation. Jonah was a master at playing games. That's all he was doing now.

"You might be wondering how I know your

name, but it wasn't difficult to figure out. I know all about Nate Locke and who you're working for. I apologize for making you cut your vacation short with your daughter. I'll make sure to send flowers for your funeral."

Salt put his hand in his pocket and Nate tensed, bringing up his weapon, but Salt only pulled out a small silver remote, no bigger than a finger.

"Relax, Agent Locke. Or should I call you Warlock. I remember you from some years back. You had quite the reputation in the CIA. Though I'd heard rumors you'd died quite horribly."

"You know what they say about rumors," Nate said.

"So it seems. Today is just as good a day for that horrible death."

"And how do you hope to accomplish that?" Eden asked. "Last I checked there were two of us and one of you."

"Well, first I am going to put a bullet in you. Right here," he said, pointing at his forehead. "You won't be able to walk away from that one, and I think it's important for Agent Locke to watch you die. He cares for you, though he's trying not to show it. Really, it's very sweet." Salt's smile was a cruel slash across his face.

"And I do owe you for the shot you took at me the other day." He flexed his shoulder where the bullet had penetrated. "It was very clever of you to come at me from the water. I didn't expect it. And clever is something you've always been, Eden. Which is just another reason it's important for you to die first."

"The minute you do he'll gun you down like the dog you are," she said coolly. "It's worth the sacrifice."

"Ahh, there's where the problem comes in," Salt said. "I've got nothing to lose here. The second my heart stops beating this whole area will blow. I've got this nifty heart monitor." He pulled back the sleeve of his jacket to expose the flesh-colored pad and digital readout of his heartbeat. "And it's connected wirelessly to enough TNT to take out a good chunk of this area the minute my heart stops beating." He shrugged. "But either way, the two of you die."

Nate caught Eden's gaze and in it he saw the finality and acceptance of what was going to happen. There was a good chance that neither of them would come out of this alive.

He heard Cal and Atticus talking on the other end of the earbud, while Cal tried to figure out a way to disarm the bomb and get everyone out alive, but he knew they were worried. The calmer Atticus's voice became the more worried he was.

"Eden," he said, seeing in her eyes the sacrifice she planned to make. "Just trust me."

She nodded once and looked back at Jonah. "If I'm going to die," she said, "then I plan to drag you with me kicking and screaming."

Salt let the gun drop down from his sleeve and into his hand, but Nate was ready for him. He shot him in the chest, just to the left of his heart. It was a killing blow that would have him bleeding out in seconds, but it would hopefully keep his heart pumping long enough for them to get the hell out of there.

Salt squeezed off two rounds as he crumpled to his knees, but they went wild.

"Run," Nate yelled, sprinting as fast as he could for the snowmobile.

Nate grabbed Eden by the arm and pulled her with him onto the closest one. He straddled it and started the engine as she climbed on behind him. There wasn't time to look back. His only thought was to go as fast as he could and get as far away as possible. He pressed on the accelerator and it took off, spraying snow up on both sides so it hit them in the face.

The sound of another gunshot seemed unusually loud over the engine, and he heard Eden whisper, "Oh, God." Her arms tightened around his waist. "He shot himself."

Nate pressed harder on the accelerator and they shot over an embankment. He could see the speck of Devil's Mining Camp at the base of the hill and he leaned forward, hoping and praying they'd be out of reach.

Seconds was all it took for the earth to rumble beneath them as the bomb detonated. The snowmobile quivered beneath his hands and the ground trembled. The earth seemed to cave in on itself, starting from the bunker and rippling outward, disintegrating everything in its path as it widened.

"Faster, faster," Eden chanted in his ear, leaning forward as if that would help with the momentum.

The sound of the explosion was delayed, and when it finally reached them the power behind it lifted them and the snowmobile and pushed them forward. They reached the bottom of the hill and sped through the narrow street between the buildings at Devil's Mining Camp and shot through to the other side. Wood creaked and snapped as what was left of the buildings crumbled into piles of rubble.

And then, as suddenly as it began, everything stopped and the world seemed to go still. Nate skidded the snowmobile to a stop and turned to look at the destruction.

"God," he whispered under his breath. Not twenty feet from where they stood was a crater in the earth at least the size of two football fields. There was nothing there but a gaping hole of darkness. Truly the end of the world.

"I think I need to tell you something important," Eden said, still clinging to his waist. He didn't want her to ever let go. That was much too close of a call.

"Yes, I think we should wait until our wedding night," he said to lighten the tension. "But maybe we could find a priest tonight. Sleeping in close quarters with you is making me crazy."

"Idiot." She choked out a laugh. "I was going to tell you I love you."

He turned to look at her and cocked a brow. "You can't take it back. We just survived the End of the World."

"Wait, she was serious about marriage?" Cal asked through the earbud. "No way is Nate getting married. He swore it off years ago."

"Shut up, Cyph. I'd like to tell the woman I'm going to marry I love her without your help."

"Buddy, you need all the help you can get," Cal said. "Another good man down."

"Maybe you could send out a helicopter to pick us up," Nate said. "I've got important plans this evening. And I don't want to be late."

"Already on the way," Atticus said. "Glad you both made it out. Oh, and Eden. Welcome to Dynamis Security."

Nate took the piece out of his ear and tossed it into the snow, and then he pulled Eden into his arms and kissed her. The End of the World was a good place to start a future.

Chapter Sixteen

Two months later...

The sun beat down on her face as she watched the waves crash along the shore. The veranda was cool in the afternoons and fans whirred lazily above her. She lounged back, unselfconscious in nothing but bikini bottoms. Her scars were on full display, but they were just part of who she was. And there was no one to see them but Nate, and he'd kissed every single one of them until she'd no longer cared they were there.

After Alaska, she wasn't sure she'd ever be warm again. But Nate had managed to find a way.

He'd been good to his word. It turned out Joe

was a licensed minister and the county clerk, so he'd issued their license and married them as soon as they'd made it back to Nome. Then Nate had called in every favor he was owed, told Atticus they could be debriefed after their honeymoon, and then he'd whisked her away to Costa Rica.

It had been two months of paradise, but she knew they couldn't hold off the rest of the world for much longer. The CIA was getting impatient to debrief her, and she couldn't keep imposing on Atticus to keep them at bay.

Nate had chosen a beautiful place—the roof was orange tile and the walls a pale stucco. It was open and airy with lots of windows to enjoy the view, and it was hidden behind an iron gate and lush trees that hid parrots and the occasional monkey. It was an oasis of complete privacy and seclusion, and the ocean was so close she only had to walk out the back door and down the short flight of stairs to be on the beach and in the water.

As soon as she'd walked inside, she'd been home. And she felt like she had a purpose again—one that she could be proud of—and a partner who would stand beside her always. Nate stimulated her mind and her body in equal measure.

As if he'd known she'd been thinking of him,

Nate came out on the veranda, wearing his swim trunks and an old tattered T-shirt.

"I feel overdressed," he said, removing his shirt.

She grinned, enjoying the sight of his body. And it was all hers. "I was just thinking about taking a swim."

"Great minds," he said, taking her hand and pulling her up from the lounger. He held her close for a few seconds before kissing her softly, and then he led her by the hand down the steps toward the water.

"I just got off the phone with Atticus," he said, his tone easy and conversational.

She arched a brow and couldn't help but smile. She knew Nate was starting to feel restless too.

"And what did Atticus have to say?" she asked.

Nate shrugged. "He's having some trouble at the embassy in South America. He needs a couple of agents to go in and pose as husband and wife so they can figure out who's selling out dignitaries from the inside."

"Hmm," she said. The cool waves lapped at her feet. "It just so happens I know a couple of agents who would do a great job at posing as a married couple."

"We must know the same people," Nate said wryly.

"We can't stay here forever," she said. "This time has been amazing. It was exactly what we needed. But we need the other too. We're not ready for retirement yet."

"I'd go crazy," he said, the relief obvious in his voice. "But I want you to take as much time as you want. You only get one honeymoon."

"Really?" she asked, brow arched teasingly. "Because I was thinking every time we come home from a job we could come back here. It's not like I can just be naked anywhere." She pushed down her bottoms and tossed them to the sand, and then she ran into the water.

She laughed as he did the same and came after her.

"You've got a deal, Agent Kane," he said, lifting her in his arms before the wave overtook her. "Have I told you how much I love my new partner?"

"No, but she sounds amazing," she said. "Maybe you could tell me now."

Midnight Clear
Coming Christmas 2023

Hank O'Hara stared out of the window in his father's office, fascinated by the bony branches of the sycamore trees that surrounded his parent's farm. Twin Peaks jutted from behind the trees—snow covered and majestic—and pregnant gray clouds frothed low and ominous, seeping into the valleys. More snow would come before morning.

It had been a wicked winter, the temperatures below freezing and the wind whipping from down the mountain and into Laurel Valley. Even the die hard skiers were giving the mountains a hard pass this winter.

He took a drink of the hot tea he'd made as he passed through the kitchen and winced when he found it cold. He had no idea how long he'd been standing at the window, thinking of the projects he had piling up or how he'd rather be outdoors than cooped up inside—even with a snowstorm coming.

"You can't hide in here forever, you know," his father said.

Hank turned from the window to see his father grinning at him from behind his massive walnut desk. His feet were propped on the edge as he leaned back in his chair, very much lord of the castle. He was a handsome man—an older version of the five sons he'd sired—with silver hair that had once been black as coal and the blue eyes of the Irish gypsies he was descended from. His body was disciplined and in excellent shape for a man in his early sixties. Farm life wasn't for the weak.

Mick O'Hara was a man's man and had managed to raise five rambunctious—and sometimes mischievous—sons to adulthood with only a handful of trips to the ER over the years. A success in Hank's opinion.

"You're doing a pretty good job of it," Hank said, tipping his cup to his father. "In fact, if I recall, you usually disappear around this time every year."

"Well, can you blame me?" Mick asked. "I built this house with my own hands. And then I added on more rooms as each of you boys came into the world. And then I added more rooms as your brothers started marrying and adding to the family. I've grown out of my own house. Where else am I supposed to go? Even the animals are tired of me sneaking out to the barn."

Hank chuckled.

"I've got all I need right here." Mick opened the bottom drawer of his desk and pulled out a bottle of expensive Irish whiskey and a box of cigars. "What do you say, my boy? Can I pour you two fingers?"

"I wouldn't say no," Hank said, accepting the short crystal glass. "But if mom smells that cigar smoke I'm not taking the wrap for you."

"Traitor," his father said. But Mick just grinned as he took out a portable fan from his desk and flipped it on before lighting his cigar.

Hank took a seat in the burgundy leather chair across from the desk and stretched out his long legs.

"You've got work on the mind," Mick said.

"How do you know?" Hank asked.

"Because if you had a woman on the mind your expression would've been different." Mick waggled his eyebrows as he took another puff from the cigar. "I've learned a thing or two in my sixty years."

Hank's mouth quirked in a half-smile, identical to his father's. "I told mom I'd take the week off and spend it with the family since everyone is here."

"A noble thing, family," Mick said. "Nothing fills your heart with pride and makes you want to take up the bottle at the same time. Next time just tell your mother no."

Hank scoffed. "You try telling mom no."

"Did that once," Mick said, remembering fondly. "Still have the scar to prove it. Quite a woman your mother."

"There you go," Hank said, nodding. "It's not that I don't want to be here. It's nice that everyone is under one roof. It's been too long. And it's been a while since I took a vacation."

"That's an understatement," Mick said. "I didn't realize you even knew the word."

"I like staying busy," Hank defended. "And busy is better than the alternative. I've got the new city hall project ready to go, and residential building has increased, even in the off-season. It's a double-edged sword. On the one hand, I really like the money. But on the other…"

"You don't want a population boom in Laurel Valley," his dad finished.

"Yeah," Hank said.

"It was bound to happen sooner or later," Mick said. "People like to build their ski chalets and bunny bungalows. Fortunately, it's short lived. Take their money, son. You know they'll only use their fancy houses a few weeks out of the year. That thin blood does no good up here."

"Good advice," Hank said.

"And maybe while you're home for the holidays you could take a look at the boiler. It's making a weird sound again."

"At least I'm useful for something," Hank said, putting his empty glass down on the desk.

"That's the spirit," Mick said, his laugh big and booming. "You know what you need?"

"I'm sure you'll tell me."

"A wife," Mick said. "Maybe a baby or two. What you're feeling is restless. Work isn't enough to fulfill you anymore. You're almost thirty-five years old."

"And with that," Hank said, coming to his feet. "I'll go look at the boiler. And I won't mention to mom about the cigar."

Mick narrowed his eyes and clamped the cigar between his teeth. "That's just downright nasty. You'd blackmail your own father."

"I think it's extortion," Hank said, laughing at the indignant look on his father's face as he left the office. He wouldn't rat the old man out. But a little fear served him right for trying to meddle in his love life.

As soon as he left the secluded space where his father's office was located, he was bombarded with a cacophony of sounds. Children laughing and screaming as they chased each other at breakneck speeds through the house, his brothers yelling at a football game, and women's laughter coming from the kitchen. And then there was him.

Hank always felt a little bit like the odd man out. He was the middle child, thirteen months younger than Simon and ten months older than Grady. And he was the last man standing. All four of his brothers were happily married. Most of them with children and it always seemed like more were always on the way.

A rather raucous shriek came from somewhere overhead and he heard a crash followed by a herd of footsteps running down the stairs.

"Harrison O'Hara," his sister-in-law Katrina yelled from the kitchen. "That better not have been you and your merry band of cousins. If you made a mess you clean it up."

There were grumbles and a bunch of, "Yes, ma'ams," as footsteps could be heard going back up the stairs.

Hank grinned. It was bedlam. Complete bedlam. He loved his family. Really, he did. It's just that there were so many of them. Everywhere he turned, there was another O'Hara in his path for him to trip over.

Hank considered himself a tolerant kind of man. But enough was enough. He hadn't had fifteen minutes to himself in the last week with his nephews and nieces underfoot. He'd exhausted every avenue of entertainment he could possibly think of—sledding, ice skating, taking the kids to get ice cream sundaes at Hoopers, and they'd played so many video games his eyes were starting to cross. He loved being the "favorite" uncle, but if he didn't get out of this place soon he was going to lose his mind. It seemed like every O'Hara in the house had something to say or argue about. And they all had to do it at top volume.

There were a bunch of manly cheers from the next room as a touchdown was scored, and his youngest brother Wyatt skidded out of the family room and ran to the kitchen at top speed, coming out seconds later with a tray of snacks and a bucket of cold drinks. The women were smart enough to know the best place the men could be was out of the kitchen while they were cooking

Christmas dinner, so they kept snacks at the ready to shove into waiting arms.

Hank's head was pounding. He was used to the commotion after all these years, but there was a reason he chose to live in the little house he'd built, secluded from the rest of the town—and better yet, the rest of the O'Haras.

"Uncle Hank!" his nephew Charlie said, cornering him in the mudroom. He had the wild-eyed look of a kid who'd had too much candy and had been playing video games too long. "Come play Mario Kart. I'm the champion. Ain't nobody that can beat me."

"Raincheck, kid," Hank said, tousling the top of his dark head. "I've gotta do a job for grandad."

Hank pulled on his ski cap and his warm lambskin jacket. His scarf was still damp from the last snowball fight, so he didn't bother with it. He pulled his gloves from his pockets slipped them on, hoping the tools he had in his truck would be enough to fix the problem. The hardware store was closed, and he'd have to drive to his shop for parts if they were needed.

"Aww, man," Charlie said, pouting pitifully. "Who am I supposed to beat now?"

On second thought, maybe a trip to his shop was exactly the escape he needed.

"Go ask your dad," Hank said.

"No way," Charlie said, expression horrified at the thought. "He's the worst. I always beat him. Besides, mom said he couldn't play anymore because he got too excited and broke her plant."

Hank's lips twitched, tucking away that bit of information for later use. "I'll tell you what. As soon as I'm done with the boiler I'll come beat you."

Charlie gave him a gap-toothed smile and held out his pudgy hand for Hank to shake. "Deal."

"Oh, Hank," his mother said, peeking into the mudroom. She looked frazzled and her cheeks were pink from the heat in the kitchen. "I've been looking everywhere for you. You're not leaving are you?"

Anne O'Hara was still one of the most beautiful women he'd ever seen. Her hair was a softer shade of red than it had been when he was a child, and it was artfully highlighted with wisps of blonde. Her skin was smooth due to a fantastic esthetician, her eyes a snapping green, and she had a voice like an angel.

She'd been on the way to Broadway stardom

when she'd met his father forty years before. Mick had been dragged kicking and screaming to the opening night of Kiss Me Kate by a guy who'd set him up with a mutual friend for a blind date. Mick hadn't had much interest in the blind date, but he'd taken one look at Anne Winslow and fought his way backstage after the show to get an introduction.

Mick got tossed out on his ear by security that night, but not before he'd gotten Anne's number. It had been instant attraction for the both of them. A once in a lifetime meeting of souls that were meant to spend eternity together. They eloped two weeks later.

Then in a very short period of times their lives and priorities changed. His mother finished the run of Kiss Me Kate about the time she found out she was pregnant with his oldest brother Arthur, and his father was sent the news that his old man had died suddenly from a tractor incident, leaving the ranch to his widow and to fend off all the wolves coming out of the woodwork to try and buy up prime real estate.

His parents had no choice but to come home. It was a sacrifice they'd both been happy to make.

Hank had grown up hearing the story of how his parents had met. Maybe it had painted an unrealistic expectation in his mind of what it would be like when he finally met the right woman. Maybe he'd passed up a woman or two who'd have made perfectly acceptable wives and mothers. But his gut just kept telling him he'd know when the time came. That's the hope he held on to.

"I was heading down to the basement," Hank said. "Dad said the boiler is acting up."

"Oh, right," she said, waving a hand in dismissal. "If it's not one thing it's another in this old house. Don't tell your father, but I wouldn't mind living out the rest of our days in one of those sleek condos you're building downtown. I heard there will even be laundry service."

"You heard right," Hank said, shocked at her confession. "I thought you loved this place."

"Some days I do," she admitted. "Today is not one of those days. I've got a boiler from the pit of Hades, fences that always need mending, creaky floors, and your father keeps escaping to the barn to smoke those cigars of his. Not to mention I've got a twenty pound turkey I've got to figure out how to shove in that ancient oven. Which is why I'm glad I caught you before you head out to look at the boiler. I need your man strength."

"Good thing you had sons instead of daughters," Hank said, pulling off his gloves and following her back into the chaos.

Cheers greeted him from his sisters-in-law as he came into the old farmhouse kitchen. The smells that greeted him would be worth every bit of inconvenience and headache in the end.

"Our hero," Katrina said.

Zoe winked, rubbing her very pregnant belly, and said, "Have I ever told you you're my favorite brother-in-law? I'm too fat to maneuver myself and a turkey in this kitchen."

"What mom needs is a new kitchen," Hattie said, giving him a look that made him very nervous. "One of those new state of the art kitchens that would fit all of us as we grow. You'd think there was someone in the family who could see to something like that."

"Hank's offered to renovate this place more times than I can count," Anne said, coming to her son's defense. "The problem is I can't decide what I want. There's too many choices. So I'll just leave it as is until I can make up my mind."

"What you need is one of those home makeover shows," Beth said, popping an olive in her mouth from one of the snack trays. Her pregnancy was just beginning to show and she was at the stage where cravings were becoming frequent and insistent.

As the newest member of the family, she wasn't always as outspoken as the others. But once she sunk her teeth into something she didn't let it go.

"Ooh, I love that idea," Zoe seconded.

Beth nodded enthusiastically. "Then they can just come in and get to know your style before kicking you out and redoing the whole place. No decisions needed."

"I thought I was here to shove a turkey in the oven," Hank said, the heat from the kitchen snaking rivulets of sweat down his back.

"Shove away, son," Anne said, pointing to the oversized roasting pan on the counter. "May the Lord be with you."

He snickered and made his way over to the oven, making sure the rack was in the right place for optimal space, and then he turned back to look at the turkey with doubt.

"Dad might have gotten a little overzealous in his turkey selection this year," Hank said.

"Not at all," Anne said. "Served him right if you ask me. Meanest turkey we've ever had here on the farm. Terrorized all the other animals. He got into the pin one day and scared chickens so bad I didn't get eggs for a week. I can't tell you how much pleasure it gave me to yank out his giblets and shove butter under his skin."

"That went darker than I thought," Hank said. "But I'll eat him anyway."

"Don't think we've forgotten about the kitchen," Hattie said. "Your dimples and boyish good looks only go so far."

He shoved the turkey in the oven with a grunt and managed to get the door closed, and then he put a hand on his lower back, mostly kidding about the muscles that were probably going to be very sore later.

"You heard the woman," Hank said, making his way back toward the door and flashing the dimples in question. "She can't make up her mind. But when she does, I'll have a crew here ready to tear this whole place apart."

"My mother told me you just hired Eloise Drake as your new designer," Beth said. "She was always a sweet girl."

"Eloise Drake?" Anne asked, her surprise evident. "I had no idea she'd moved back to Laurel Valley. Tragic what happened to her parents. I always wondered where she ended up. Why didn't you tell me you hired her?"

The look his mother gave him was accusing, and he wondered what he was missing.

"Do you want to come on as the head of HR?" he asked. "Then you'll be the first to know who comes on staff."

"Don't be a smart aleck," she said, flicking a dish towel at him.

"I posted the job last month and Eloise sent in her resume," Hank said, shrugging. "She was the most qualified for the job. What's the big deal? What am I missing?"

He didn't mention that the moment Eloise had walked into his office for the interview it felt like he'd been punched in the solar plexus. He'd had a hard time drawing in a breath for the entire half hour she'd sat across from him. But she hadn't looked familiar, and he certainly hadn't realized she'd grown up in Laurel Valley.

"She graduated in my class," Beth said. "So she would've been several years behind you. Her parents were Richard and Lana Drake."

Hank winced sympathetically. He'd been finishing up an apprenticeship in Denver when he'd heard the news about the murder/suicide of the Drakes.

Richard had been the DA for more than a decade and Lana had served on many of the committees that made Laurel Valley what it was today. They were wealthy and untouchable. At least that was the thought. The scandal had made national news as it came out that Richard was about to be indicted for everything from money laundering to extortion, and he more than likely would have spent the rest of his life in jail.

Richard must have gotten wind of the indictment because the last time they were seen was leaving a charity gala on Christmas Eve. From there Richard drove them up into the mountains toward their ski cabin, but he drove them right off the side of the mountain instead. There'd been no skid marks and the weather and roads were clear. The car had exploded on impact, killing Richard instantly, but the medical examiner had found a .22 in Lana's temple.

Hank remembered there'd been mention of a teenage daughter home from college for Christmas break. He hadn't put it together when he'd met Eloise. He'd thought she'd just been nervous about the interview, but he realized now the kind of courage it took to come back to the place where you'd lived out your worst nightmares.

"Poor girl," Anne said. "She's going to need good friends when she gets back into town."

"She's already back," Beth said. "Mama said she moved into one of Hank's condo's downtown. I was planning to stop by and see her after Christmas."

"This has to be a hard time of year for her," Anne said. "The anniversary of her parent's death. And no one to spend Christmas with on top of it. You should invite her here, Hank."

Hank's brows shot up and he felt a slight panic at the suggestion. "Me? Why me? I've only met her once."

"Don't be ridiculous," Anne said, flicking him again with the towel. "She works for O'Hara Construction now. That means she's one of the family."

Hank sighed. His mother had that look on her face that meant there was nothing anyone could do to sway her otherwise. "Fine, I'll invite her. Can I go fix the boiler now?"

"Be my guest," Anne said. "And thanks for shoving that devil turkey into the oven for me."

Hank chuckled as he put his gloves back on and headed out the back door and into peace and quiet.

Pre-order today from any retailer where books are sold!

About the Author

Liliana Hart is a *New York Times*, *USA Today*, and Publisher's Weekly bestselling author of more than eighty titles. After starting her first novel her freshman year of college, she immediately became addicted to writing and knew she'd found what she was meant to do with her life. She has no idea why she majored in music.

Since publishing in June 2011, Liliana has sold more than ten-million books. All three of her series have made multiple appearances on the New York Times list.

Liliana can almost always be found at her computer writing, hauling five kids to various activities, or spending time with her husband. She calls Texas home.

If you enjoyed reading this book, I would appreciate it if you would help others enjoy this book too.

Recommend it. Please help other readers find this book by recommending it to friends, readers' groups and discussion boards.

Review it. Please tell other readers why you liked this book by reviewing.

Connect with me online:
www.lilianahart.com

Also by Liliana Hart

JJ Graves Mystery Series

Dirty Little Secrets

A Dirty Shame

Dirty Rotten Scoundrel

Down and Dirty

Dirty Deeds

Dirty Laundry

Dirty Money

A Dirty Job

Dirty Devil

Playing Dirty

Dirty Martini

Dirty Dozen

Dirty Minds

Addison Holmes Mystery Series

Whiskey Rebellion

Whiskey Sour

Whiskey For Breakfast

Whiskey, You're The Devil

Whiskey on the Rocks

Whiskey Tango Foxtrot

Whiskey and Gunpowder

Whiskey Lullaby

The Scarlet Chronicles

Bouncing Betty

Hand Grenade Helen

Front Line Francis

The Harley and Davidson Mystery Series

The Farmer's Slaughter

A Tisket a Casket

I Saw Mommy Killing Santa Claus

Get Your Murder Running

Deceased and Desist

Malice in Wonderland

Tequila Mockingbird

Gone With the Sin

Grime and Punishment

Blazing Rattles

A Salt and Battery

Curl Up and Dye

First Comes Death Then Comes Marriage

Box Set 1

Box Set 2

Box Set 3

The Gravediggers

The Darkest Corner

Gone to Dust

Say No More

Printed in Great Britain
by Amazon